# BEST MAN

## A GAY CUCKOLD WEDDING STORY

JACK HORNWOOD

Best Man
A Gay Cuckold Wedding Story

Jack Hornwood

3<sup>rd</sup> Edition
Copyright © 2021 Jack Hornwood
ISBN: 978-1-99-117751-3
Written in Aotearoa

www.jackhornwood.com

## A MESSAGE FROM THE AUTHOR

This book is fiction, and this story is fantasy.

For me, writing erotica has been a way of exploring the things that turn me on but that I couldn't, wouldn't or shouldn't do in real life. It's a space to enjoy the fantasy without anyone having to experience the consequences of trying these things in real life.

Cuckolding is a complicated kink, and sometimes the things that turn you on the most are also the things that hurt the most. In a fictional story I can go all out, make it as brutal as I want, and just enjoy it as a fantasy. And obviously I hope you enjoy it too.

But don't take it as endorsement for treating the people in your real life like the people in this book. In real life cuckolding requires trust and communication. Everyone has different boundaries between what's hot because it hurts, and what just hurts too much.

So if you're going to try this kind of stuff at home, talk to your partner about what you want to try. Check in to keep making sure you have their enthusiastic consent. Set boundaries and stick to them unless you make a joint decision, together, to shift them.

Look after the people you care about, and make sure they know you respect them no matter where your kinks take you.

# Chapter 1

# The Proposal

I FIDGETED WITH THE RING BOX, TURNING IT around and around in my pocket. I'd pry it open just a little bit, then let it snap shut, then turn it around again. Every minute or so I'd start to take it out of my pocket to look at it, but then catch myself and stop. I had to make sure I didn't take it out of my pocket; I didn't know when Josh would show up, and I didn't want to ruin this whole night by having him catch me with the ring out.

For about the thousandth time I second-guessed whether he'd like the one I chose. It had been hard to make a decision; everything either looked too showy and ornate and effete, or else too plain to do justice to the gravity of what it represented. I think I'd chosen well. I hoped I had. Oh well, too late to change it now.

I'd been saving for the ring, and for the wedding, since before the marriage equality law had even passed. I didn't want to have one of those engagements that went on for so long that it began to seem like neither party had any intention of actually following through with a wedding. I wanted to be in a position where I was at least close to being able to afford the wedding before I popped the question, so we could set a date that resembled the foreseeable future. It had been hard to save for it; Josh and I were saving up to convert the shed in the back of our garden into a home office, so that took most of our left-over money at the moment. It had been hard to discreetly hide a bit extra away for the wedding, but I'd managed a decent amount so far.

I'd been a bundle of nerves ever since I'd decided that it was time to take the plunge and booked this weekend out of town to pop the question. When Josh had asked what the occasion was, I must have been entirely unconvincing when I told him it was just because I wanted a break from work. But he hadn't dug any deeper. Every day of our holiday I'd been on edge, worrying that I was going to let something slip and ruin the surprise. It was probably stupid to worry; Josh probably knew that it would only be a matter of time until I proposed, and the instant I'd told him about this trip I'm sure he'd probably put two and two together. I can be pretty predictable sometimes.

Still, I wanted this to be the perfect unexpected surprise. A magical night he'd look back on forever.

Having made the decision, I was also terrified that something was going to go horribly wrong with the big moment. As though, having officially made the decision that I wanted to spend the rest of my life with Josh, he'd suddenly realise he didn't want me after all and would turn me down. But I think that ultimately the nerves had been a good thing; it meant I was more attentive to his needs, more ready to examine my own behaviour when I made him annoyed or upset. And the couple of times that he'd had a bull around to fuck him in our bed, the extra anxiety of losing him had made my cuckold libido rage even harder than usual.

As I saw Josh wander up the beach to the restaurant, my stomach jumped with nerves, but I couldn't help smiling from ear to ear. He was so fucking stunning. Today his short shorts showed off his slender, tanned legs, and his scoop-necked t-shirt revealed just enough of his smooth, golden collarbone to make me want to reach out and touch it. He was slim and toned — a total twink — with smooth honey skin, and jet-black hair and stubble. As he saw me he smiled his wide, super-model smile, and waved.

He strolled up to the restaurant, and I stood up to meet him. I took him in my arms and kissed him. Slowly, tenderly, maybe a little too long for this public spot we were in. "Hey, handsome," I greeted him. "How was your nap?"

"I couldn't sleep in the end," he replied, sitting down at the table across from me. "I read my book for a while. Where did you end up going?"

"Just for a walk. I just needed to chill on my own for a bit." Honest, but evading any further explanation. "You ready to eat?"

"So hungry," Josh said, clutching his stomach in faux star-vation. "You?"

I was so nervous I didn't think I could eat a thing. "Yup. Famished."

We'd spent almost every minute of the last couple of days together, so we didn't have much news to catch each other up on. Josh talked about the book he'd been reading, and told me about the hermit crab he'd seen on the beach earlier. We talked about our plans for our final day here — we hadn't taken the kayaks or the paddle-boards out yet, which we were keen to do before we had to leave.

"Honey, I got on the apps before," Josh told me."I found a guy staying here, in the main hotel. He said he could be up for fucking me later tonight. You keen?"

I felt my dick respond to the question, starting to thicken slightly. At the same time I felt a little disappointed though, which was unusual for me. Even though I love to watch him get fucked, I guess I'd been hoping that this night in particular would just be about the two of us.

"He's about your age. Looks pretty fit. Likes the idea of having you watch." He paused for a second, seeming to sense my uncertainty. "We don't have to though, no big deal."

"Maybe, let's see how we feel later?"

Dinner was phenomenal, as always at this restaurant. Afterwards the waiter came by to ask if we wanted dessert, but tonight neither of us were keen — me because I was still a bundle of nerves. We settled up the bill, and decided to go for a walk down by the beach.

The sun was just starting to set as we set off down the beach. Shades of pink, peach and orange lit up the horizon. It was perfect. A moment exactly like I'd pictured in my mind since the day I'd first realised I was in love with Josh.

I gently grabbed onto Josh's arm, to stop him and turn him to face me. "Josh, there's something I want to say to you."

"What is it?" For a moment a look of concern flashed over his face.

I took a deep breath, and tried to remember all the things I'd dreamed I'd say in this moment. "Josh, you are everything to me. You've brought me so much love, so much fun, so much intense excitement. I never thought I'd meet anyone like you; I never dreamed for a second that I could be so lucky to ever meet a man as perfect and as beautiful as you are. You've made my life amazing, and I never ever want to lose you. I want to spend my whole life with you."

I dropped to one knee — clichéd, I know, but it seemed right in the moment. I reached into my pocket, and pulled out the ring box. "Joshua Castillo, it would mean the whole world to me if you agreed to be my husband."

Josh looked shocked for a second. For a moment my stomach started to sink as I panicked that I'd misjudged horribly. But then a grin spread slowly across his face.

"Of course," he replied. Then, "What took you so long?"

It took a couple of seconds for the words to sink in. *He actually said yes.* Of course he said yes. How could I have even doubted it? I felt a smile start to bubble out of me, rising from my chest and taking over every muscle of my face without any conscious intent, or ability to stop it, on my part.

Josh put out his hand. "So you gonna put that ring on it, or not?"

My hand was shaking uncontrollably as I slid the ring onto his finger. Once it was on, I just stared at it for I don't know how long. The ring I bought, the ring that signified his willingness to be my husband, right there on his hand. This had actually just happened.

I looked up and saw that he was grinning just as hard as I was. I got up off my knee, swept him into my arms and kissed him. "I love you so much."

For a while we just stood there, in each other's arms, making out in the golden glow of the sunset. Eventually I stopped, pausing to study his beautiful face as I pulled away. I took his hand, and together we walked slowly down the beach. As I looked out at the last stripe of pink as the sun descended, and then back at the face of my husband-to-be in the dim light, I couldn't believe how lucky I was.

I realised then that I had no idea what to do next. Everything had led to this moment, and I hadn't given any thought to what to do after it was over. "What do you want to do now, babe? Do you want to arrange to meet that guy you were talking about?"

Josh thought about for a second, then shook his head. "Nah. I'd rather be fucked by..." He grinned. "...my fiancé."

I lit up, and kissed him. "We should get going then. Should I call a taxi?"

"No," he said. His grin got bigger, and his eyes darted sideways - the look he always gave when he was contemplating mischief. "I want to get fucked by my fiancé, right here on the beach." With that he turned, and started running up towards the dunes. I stood and watched for a few seconds, in awe at how lucky I was right now.

"You coming?" he called back to me.

# CHAPTER 2

## THE BULL

JOSH'S PHONE BUZZED ON THE TABLE. HE PICKED IT up and read the message. "He's in a cab," he told me. "He's not far away so he'll be here in a few minutes."

I was excited; it had been a few weeks since I'd gotten to watch Josh get fucked. Things had been really good lately, and the two of us had been fucking like rabbits ever since the night he accepted my proposal. But getting cuckolded was a whole different ball game. It made me horny like nothing else, and I'd been missing it.

The guy was an out-of-towner here on business. That was the best kind of hookup because we didn't need to worry about the possibility we'd see him around after — or even worse, that we'd realise too late that it was someone we already knew. I'd seen a photo of him on Josh's phone; he was handsome, really handsome. Early forties, with short hair and a cropped beard, both of which were dark with flecks of silver. He had a strong jawline, and hard features that communicated a refusal to take any nonsense. Without trying to project too much of my own fantasy onto his photo, it was hard not to assume that he was a total alpha male. Dominant, authoritative, strong. I'd asked to see pics of his body and his cock, but Josh had just shaken his head and said, "I want you to see for yourself in person. Don't worry, you'll be impressed."

As I waited those last few minutes for him to arrive I checked the bedroom to make sure everything was in order. It was not too bad, everything was pretty tidy. I noticed that the sheets were the same ones that had been on the bed for almost a week though. That wouldn't do. Not so much because it would give a bad impression, more because after Josh got fucked in our bed I liked to sleep in the sweat and cum stains for as long as possible. It would be a shame if we had to put clean sheets on the bed in a day or two's time.

I quickly stripped the bed and grabbed some new sheets out of the cupboard. I made the bed and put the duvet cover back on as fast as I could. I was just putting the last pillowcase on when I heard the knock at the door. As I smoothed out the duvet I heard Josh open the door and greet our visitor. I quickly grabbed the condoms and lube from the drawer and set them on the bedside table.

They talked for a moment but I couldn't quite hear what they said. But then I heard Josh say "Come on through to the bedroom,"

He entered the room, and when I laid eyes on the man who accompanied him my dick twitched instantly in my pants. For a second I just stood there and took in the sight of him. He was tall, over six foot, easily a head taller than me and a good few inches on Josh. He was built like a brick shithouse, too. He had a big chest, thick neck, broad shoulders, and muscular arms. He was wearing a t-shirt and gym shorts, and the bulge of a huge cock was unmistakeable.

"Brian, this is my boyfriend, Simon," Josh introduced me.

"Fiancé," I corrected him, with a nervous smile. I extended my hand. "Nice to meet you."

Brian took a step towards me, and as he did I saw that big

dick swing in his shorts. He took my hand and shook it firmly. "Hey. So I hear you like to watch your boy take cock."

My heart raced and my dick jumped. A lot of the guys we'd found in the past were just interested in fucking Josh, and didn't really care whether I was around to watch. But occasionally we found a bull who was just as into cuckolding me as he was into fucking Josh. The way Brian said that, and the way he looked at me as he said it, I could tell he was into the idea of fucking a guy with a cuckold partner.

"Yeah," I admitted, both bashfully and proudly at the same time, if that's possible.

"You're in for a treat then," Brian replied. He turned and looked at Josh. "Shall we, then?"

"Where do you guys want me?" I asked.

Neither of them looked at me; their eyes were locked on each other, the anticipation obvious. "Over there," Brian gestured absently. As I sat down on my stool in the corner, he put his arms gently around Josh's waist and kissed him on the lips.

"Get your clothes off, boy," he ordered Josh. "I want to see what I'm going to be playing with tonight."

Josh obliged, first pulling off his t-shirt over his head. He threw it on the floor, then started to pull down his shorts, never taking his eyes off Brian. When he was down to his underwear, Brian took Josh's balls in his hand and massaged them slowly. "Turn around."

Josh turned around, exposing his firm, round ass in his briefs. Brian ran a finger gently down his crack, and then massaged his taint through the fabric of his underwear. That made Josh moan.

"Good boy," Brian said in a low growl. "Sounds like you want to get fucked tonight."

"Yes, please," Josh whispered.

"Not yet though. You gotta get me ready first." He pulled

down his gym shorts, which had nothing on underneath. From where I was standing behind him, his ass looked firm and muscular, as were his thighs.

Josh looked down at his cock, and let out a gasp. "Fuck," he whispered. He reached out and touched it gently.

I wanted to get a look at that cock. So I got up off my stool and inched my way towards them until I could get a decent view. Fuck, it was a monster. It was still mostly soft, but even mostly soft it was about as long as mine is when it's hard. And it was thick and meaty, too, thicker than mine when it's hard. Josh fondled it, weighed it in his hand. With the other hand he reached for Brian's big, full, low-hanging balls, and started to massage them.

"That's good, boy," Brian growled.

Josh dropped to his knees. He lifted Brian's weighty cock out of the way, and began to lick his balls. He let his cock rest on his face as he licked; the tip reached all the way to his hairline. As Josh licked and kissed his nut sack, I could see Brian's cock begin to swell and stiffen. As it got harder, Josh put a hand around it — his hand could barely wrap the whole way around — and slowly jacked it up and down.

"You like those nuts, boy?" Brian asked.

"Yes," came the muffled reply as he licked and sucked with more enthusiasm.

"Good. Now why don't you taste that cock."

Josh licked the entire way up his massive shaft, his tongue lingering at Brian's piss-slit. He flicked his tongue across it, and around it, and then slid his mouth over the fat mushroom tip.

"You like that cock, boy?"

"Yes," he replied. "It's beautiful. It's so big."

"Ha, been a while since you had a cock this big then?"

"Yeah. I don't even remember how long," Josh admitted.

"So your boyfriend's not packing anything like this, then?" Brian asked.

"Nothing like this."

Brian turned to look at me. "Let's see it, cuck. Show me the little dick this boy's been putting up with all this time."

He watched as I anxiously started to unzip my jeans. Josh didn't bother to look up, he was completely consumed by Brian's cock, and he was getting it deeper and deeper down his throat with each motion.

My underwear already had a wet patch where I'd started to drip precum from watching them. I pulled out my erect cock, and took my hands off it so Brian could get a proper look.

"I see what you mean, boy," he said to Josh, but still looking me in the face. "That's not a real cock. I'm surprised you let that baby dick anywhere near you."

That made my cock even harder.

"It's your lucky day, cuck. You're gonna see how a real man with a real cock fucks your boy."

With that he grabbed Josh by the armpits, and lifted him up off his cock and into a standing position. Then he threw him down on the bed, pulled off his t-shirt and got on top of him. Pinning him down, he kissed him some more, then kissed his ears and neck, working his way down to his collarbone and then his chest. He sucked on Josh's nipples, which drove Josh wild; he writhed underneath Brian until Brian grabbed him by the wrists and held him down. Then Brian licked and sucked some more, and bit Josh's nipple, causing him to yelp in pain.

"You like that, boy?"

"I love it! Don't stop!"

Brian licked and bit his nipple, holding him down while he struggled and moaned. "You're getting all worked up, boy," he laughed. "You want to get fucked, don't you?"

"Yes!"

"Good boy. You gotta wait a bit longer yet though." He kissed his way down Josh's happy trail, reached into his jocks and pulled out his erect cock. He squeezed it, and jerked it.

"You're already leaking," he observed. He grabbed the waist of Josh's jocks and pulled them down, then got back on top of him and spread his legs apart, resting the head of his cock against Josh's ass.

"Fuck, that feels so good. I want it inside of me," Josh moaned.

"You gonna beg?"

"Fuck, daddy, please!"

"How 'bout you, you gonna beg too?"

I was so absorbed in the performance that it took me a second or two to realise that question was aimed at me. Fuck. He wanted me to beg. I could feel my dick twitch and release a little more precum into my already soaked boxers.

"Fuck him, please," I said, in what was almost a whisper.

"What was that?"

"I, I want you to fuck him, please."

"I want to know you mean it," Brian told me. "I'm not fucking him till I'm sure that both of you need me to. Your boyfriend here needs me to, don't you boy?"

"Fuck," Josh said, the desperation clear in his voice. "I want you to fuck me so bad. Simon, hurry up and tell him you want him to fuck me."

This exchange was making my dick ache. It was new territory for me; this guy was a natural-born bull, the way he was making me not just sit back and let my fiancé be fucked, but to actually ask for it myself. "Please," I said, this time with purpose. "Will you fuck him for me? We both need it."

Brian sneered at me for a second, pleased with himself. Then he looked Josh in the eyes and asked him quietly, almost tenderly, "You ready for me?"

Josh nodded emphatically. They kissed again.

I decided to make myself useful. I grabbed a condom and the bottle of lube, and brought them over. The two of them were lost in each other, Josh pinned down under Brian's body as they made out. I just stood there and waited till the appropriate moment.

Eventually they stopped kissing, and Brian noticed I was there. I held out the condom and the lube for him.

He took the lube from my hand. He looked at the condom, then at me. I could tell what he was thinking, and I felt the hairs on the back of my neck prickle at the thought of having to try and lay down the law to a man like him who I could barely handle looking in the eyes.

He took the condom from my hand, and I felt a rush of relief that there would be no confrontation. I walked across the room, dragging my stool across to where I could get a better view of the two of them. Then I sat down for the show.

Brian held up the condom, dangling it above Josh. "Your boyfriend wants me to use this," he told him.

Neither of them said anything.

"Do you want me to use this?" he asked Josh.

Silence. Josh briefly looked over at me, just for a second, then away again.

"Do you want me to use this?" he asked again, this time rubbing the tip of his cock slowly and gently against Josh's hole. "Or do you want to feel me, inside you, skin on skin?"

Josh didn't say a word. But he looked over at me again, this time longer, and with a look of pleading in his eyes. It was obvious what he wanted.

There was a long pause, like a standoff before a gunfight. I was too terrified — with good reason — to give them the okay, but just as terrified that Josh might just go ahead and say yes anyway. The thought of Josh disregarding my wishes, and going ahead with it, made my heart race and my dick swell even more than they already were. It was almost as hot as the thought of Brian fucking Josh raw and breeding him in front of me.

Without saying a word Josh was practically begging me,

just with the expression in his eyes. He began to draw a short breath, and as he did so I could see the look on his face change. Guilt, and resolve. And I knew what he was about to say.

But Brian broke the spell right at that moment. "Kidding," he said. With a grin he ripped the condom wrapper open with his teeth, took it out, and started rolling it onto his cock.

Josh looked back at me, apologetically. I knew what had just happened. Without actually fucking Josh raw, he'd proven that he could if he wanted to, regardless of what I thought.

It was a struggle to get the condom on; it was a large but it was nowhere near big enough for his cock. He had to stretch it open with his hands and then try to get it on inch by inch, like someone trying to cram a duvet back into the carry bag it came in from the store. Eventually it ripped, and he pulled it off, frustrated.

I ran to the bedside table and frantically fossicked around for something bigger. I could feel the pressure, knowing that Josh was desperate to be fucked, and feeling like I was the one who created the inconvenience by expecting them to use a condom in the first place. I eventually found an XXL, and quickly handed it to Brian. With a bit of manoeuvring he managed to get it on successfully, and he lubed both his cock and Josh's hole.

I sat down once again on my stool.

"Now, looks like we can get back into it, huh boy?"

"Please!" Josh sounded desperate. "Put it in me, please!"

Brian lined his cock up against Josh's hole, gently teasing it. He lifted Josh's legs into the air, and pushed them back so his knees were up against his chest. Then, looking Josh in the eyes, he slowly started to push his cock in, just a tiny bit.

Josh moaned. "Fuck. Yeah."

Brian pushed it in further, past the tip. I could see Josh's ass start to stretch around it. He winced, then slowly exhaled.

As the air left his mouth, Brian pushed a little further, his cock slowly disappearing inch by inch.

"Fuck! Fuck! Fuck!" Josh was getting higher and higher pitched the further in Brian's cock went. His eyes were clenched closed. For a second I thought he was going to tell Brian to stop.

Brian stopped pushing, and just held his cock in place. "You alright, boy?"

Josh nodded, taking a few deep breaths. "Yeah. It feels good. It's just so fucking *big*."

"You take a second, and tell me when you want me to keep going. Or tell me if you want me to stop."

"No!" Josh was emphatic. "Don't stop. It feels fucking good, even though it hurts."

They held almost still for a few seconds, Brian kissing Josh's neck as Josh's breathing returned to normal. Eventually Josh whispered, "Okay."

Brian withdrew, just an inch. Then he pushed his cock back in. Slowly, it passed the point it had gotten to before. Then further, another inch. Then another. He stopped, held it for a second, pulled back a little. Then in again. This time in one long, slow motion he pushed past the furthest point, and Josh's hole swallowed up his entire cock, right down to the balls.

Josh let out an involuntary wail. "Oh, god!" He grabbed Brian's face, drew it towards him, and kissed him fervidly.

With their lips locked together, Josh's legs pinned against his chest by Brian's body, Brian's hips began to slowly thrust in and out as he fucked him. With each thrust in, Josh let out a little groan that was muffled by their kiss. Each time Brian pulled out I was reminded just how long his cock was, and with every thrust I could picture just how far up unto Josh it was reaching. He was touching parts of Josh's anatomy that I'd never reached before.

Gradually Brian picked up the pace. He pulled himself up off Josh so he was on his knees. Wrapping his arms around each of Josh's legs and using them for leverage, he started to pound Josh's ass harder. Any pain Josh might have felt at first seemed long gone. He wailed every time Brian's cock hit him deep, and he was a breathy, gasping mess. But it was obvious he was loving it.

My dick was so hard it hurt. I rubbed it through the fabric of my trousers until I couldn't help myself anymore. Watching Josh get pounded like that — harder than I'd ever pounded him — was so incredibly hot.

I slowly slid my hand down my trousers, and took a firm grip of my cock. While I started to stroke it I watched Brian's cock intensely as it slid effortlessly in and out of Josh's ass in long strokes; I thought about that feeling, and how different it would feel with a cock as thick as his.

Brian glanced over at me. He scowled. "No touching!" he barked.

Flustered, I quickly removed my hand and stammered an apology. I wanted so badly to take my dick in my hand again, but it turned me on so much that he wanted to control when I could touch it.

He grinned at me. "Not until I say."

I nodded. I sat on my hands, partly to demonstrate that I was willing to follow orders, and partly because I didn't know if I could stop myself jerking off otherwise.

That exchange had disrupted their rhythm. But Brian used that as a chance to change things up. He pulled out, his big, hard dick bouncing around as he stood up. "On your knees, boy." It was obviously an order, but he gave it with the firm, gentle manner of a coach sharing his wisdom with his trainee.

Josh obediently got on all fours, ass presented to Brian. He slowly ran his hand down his ass crack, making him whimper when it brushed across his tender, stretched hole. Then he leaned in and whispered, "Not this way. Turn around, face him."

Josh did what he was told, shuffling around ninety degrees so he was facing me. It was the first time he'd bothered to look at me since Brian started fucking him. He gave me a grin, knowing how much I'd be getting off right now from the torment.

Brian climbed onto the bed, on his knees, and positioned himself behind Josh. I couldn't see his cock from here, but I could tell by the way he was slowly moving his hips that he must be rubbing the tip of his cock lightly against Josh's hole. Josh closed his eyes, breathed in deep, and exhaled in a blissful sigh.

"You ready for me?" Brian asked.

"Yes," he groaned.

Brian looked at me. "You watching?" he asked. "I want you to see his face when I make him cum."

I nodded. That self-assured confidence, not doubting for a second that he could make Josh cum just from fucking him. For a second I wondered if he'd be in for disappointment: only a few guys had ever managed that. But something told me that he'd succeed where I always failed.

"Good. And I want to see your face when I cum in him, too."

My dick clenched and released, and I could feel a little more precum escaping.

I looked at Brian's face. He smiled. This cocky smirk, a bit of a chuckle. Then concentration as he manoeuvred his big cock. I looked at Josh's face, and I could see on it the moment that Brian entered him. He tilted his head back, closed his eyes tightly into what looked like a grimace. He took a sharp, deep intake of breath, made a pained little squeak. Brian pulled out, then thrust in deep again. Josh let out his breath in a yelp, and opened his eyes wide with a look of utter shock. "Oh god!" he yelled.

Brian pulled out then thrust in again. Harder, this time. Josh yelped again, fixed his wide eyes onto mine. "Oh god!" He let his head droop, like he was overcome with the feeling of it, and started to take deep, raspy breaths as Brian started fucking him hard again

The sight of Josh being fucked well has always been one of the most beautiful, wondrous things I've ever seen. But I couldn't help from fixing my stare onto Brian's face instead as he fucked my fiancé. Brian's face went from a look of thoughtful concentration — like he was studying the effects of his cock in Josh — to a look of relaxed pleasure, to that same cocky smirk every time he looked at me.

Brian fucked Josh forcefully, making him wail with every thrust. Josh was crying out in time with Brian's thrusts, and I could see his cock was rock hard and leaking, although he never touched it. After a while — god knows how long — Brian slowed down, and Josh finally had a chance to get his breath back. I could tell he was still fucking him deep, but now it was in smooth, slow strokes.

Brian fixed his gaze on me. "You like watching me fuck your boy?" he asked.

I nodded emphatically.

"I bet it makes you fucking hard," he continued.

I nodded again. He already knew the answer, obviously. He was playing with me, and I loved it.

"How long will you last?" he asked, "If I let you touch it?"

God, I was desperate to touch it. It had been hard, pulsing, for so long now, and I wanted to feel my hand on it so badly. "I don't know. Not long," I admitted.

"Touch it," he ordered, in time as he thrust deep into Josh and made him cry out again.

I reached for my trousers.

"Don't take it out. I don't want to have to look at it."

I slid my hand into my underpants, and finally took my hard cock in my hand. It felt so good, too good. I knew I wouldn't last long.

"Do you want your cuck boyfriend to cum?" he leaned in and whispered to Josh.

He didn't open his eyes. "I don't care," he gasped raggedly and absently, as though he hadn't even really comprehended the question. "Just keep fucking me."

Hearing that suddenly got me closer. I kept my hand still on my cock, not wanting to move it, but hoping that if I stopped jerking it I wouldn't shoot my load just yet.

Brian was now almost on top of Josh. His chest was resting on Josh's back, and he had one arm around Josh's neck in a loose choke-hold, the other arm supporting his weight. His chin was resting right on Josh's shoulder, and he kissed his neck and his earlobe. Josh was slowly starting to sink down onto the bed from his hands and knees.

"Tell me how much you like daddy's cock," Brian coaxed.

"Fuck," Josh seemed lost for words, almost exhausted. "Fuck, I love it. Fuck. I'm... Fuck. It's... Fuck. It's the best I've ever... Fuck."

I could tell Josh was close. But I was closer. I felt the orgasm well up in me as the words *best I've ever* echoed in my ears. I felt the muscles in my dick clench and release, clench and release, and I let out an almost inaudible groan as I felt the cum spill out, all over my hand and into the fabric of my underpants.

It only took a second for the familiar sense of shame and regret to sweep over me, and it was suddenly like I was transported into a different room — one filled with the horror of having my fiancé realise how much he preferred this man who fucked him better than I could.

"Show me how much you like it," Brian whispered in

Josh's ear. He suddenly slowed right down, but made sure the next slow pump went in as deep as it possibly could. "Show me how this cock makes you feel."

Josh moaned like the feeling was unbearable. "Fuck!" He clenched his eyes shut, and I knew what was coming. I looked at his cock just in time to see it pulse and shoot out its seed. The first rope of it shot so far it missed the bed and landed on the floor. It was followed by another, then another, then another, all landing in a trail on the bed. Josh let out a colossal sigh and collapsed onto the bed.

Brian looked pleased. He wasn't done though, He continued to slowly, gently fuck Josh as he whispered to him, "Did you like that boy?"

"So much," Josh sighed, his face buried in the sheets.

"You want me to cum?"

"Yes."

"You want to feel daddy cum in your ass?"

"Yes. Please."

Brian looked up at me and grinned, mischievously, as he whispered to Josh, "You wish I was about to breed you, boy?"

"Yes!" Josh's muffled reply had an air of desperation to it. He lifted his head and turned it as far around as he could, so Brian could kiss him.

"You wish I could fill you up, don't you."

"Yes." Josh kissed him again.

"Tell me what you want."

"I want to feel your cum in my ass," Josh begged.

Brian looked and me and smiled, the satisfaction emanating from him. With one more deep, hard thrust, he let out a deep, animal growl as he came.

Josh sighed in appreciation. Brian pumped a couple more times as his ejaculation continued. Then he took a deep breath, kissed Josh on the neck, and whispered, "Next time."

They lay there for a minute, elated and exhausted, Brian

still on top of and inside Josh. Eventually though he pulled out and got up off the bed. The condom was still on his cock, full and heavy. He carefully pulled it off without spilling anything, held it by the neck, and presented to me. "Go do something with this."

I gingerly took the condom from him, not sure what to do. "I... I'll just go put this in the wastebasket in the bath-room," I announced. Although no one seemed to be paying any attention to what I said; Brian had sat back down on the bed and was gently massaging Josh's back, as Josh smiled blissfully.

I walked down the hall to the bathroom. When I was in there, alone, I paused. I studied the condom. It was so full. Much fuller than I'd ever left one.

I stepped on the foot lever that opened the lid of the waste-basket. But before I could bring myself to throw it away, I put it up to my nose and breathed in deeply. It felt good, breathing in the smell of a real man's seed. Before I could really think about what I was doing, I was lifting the condom above my head and pouring the contents into my mouth. It felt thick, viscous, when it hit my tongue. It tasted salty. I ran my fingers down the length of it to squeeze out every last drop onto my tongue, and when I was sure I'd got everything I could, I swallowed.

I felt my dick stir a little again. But I knew it wasn't going to do much, and it could wait.

I threw the empty condom into the bin, and went back to the bedroom.

I found them in the same position I left them: Brian sitting on the bed, massaging Josh's back as he lay sleepily on the bed. They were having a conversation about some theatre production they'd both seen but I'd never heard of. I quietly excused myself and went to the kitchen to get glasses of water.

When I returned with water, they still hadn't moved. Now

they were talking about some film which, once again, I'd never heard of but they both seemed to know well. I handed Brian a glass of water, which he took absently without acknowledging me. I set Josh's glass down on the bedside table. I sat down on the bed next to them, unsure of whether I was going to be part of their conversation or not. As they talked, I was distracted by the cold, wet feeling in my groin where my cum had been absorbed into the fabric of my underpants.

After about twenty minutes, when there was finally a gap in the conversation that had by now meandered across several films, directors, historical moments and cities — all without either of them saying a word to me — I conspicuously yawned, stretched, and said, "Boy, I guess it's getting pretty late." I needed Brian to go. I was bored, embarrassed, and genuinely tired too.

Brian looked at me and chuckled silently, amused by my blatant attempt to get rid of him.

Josh looked up sleepily. "That's a shame, I was enjoying this. I guess it is late, though." I was relieved, until he followed that by suggesting, "You could stay over if you want."

Brian looked even more amused, probably because my face gave away exactly what I was thinking. He let the suggestion hang there for several seconds, lording it over me, before he finally said, "Nah, I'd better get home. Thanks for the offer though." He shot me another grin, the meaning of which was obvious: *I could take your bed for the night if I wanted to.*

He got up and put on his clothes. Josh pulled himself up off the bed, and gave him a long, deep kiss. "Thanks for that," he said to him. "It was amazing. I haven't been fucked that good in months. Years, maybe."

"Whenever you want it." Brian slapped him on the ass and gave him another quick kiss. "Sleep well."

He turned and walked from the room. I thought for a second that he wasn't going to acknowledge me at all, but he turned in the doorway and gave me another grin. "See you next time." Then he turned and walked out into the hallway.

"Bye," I called out meekly after him.

Josh climbed into bed, still slick with sweat and lube. He must be exhausted, he didn't even go brush his teeth, let alone clean the sex off him. I wasn't complaining though; I'd be enjoying these soiled sheets for several nights to come.

# CHAPTER 3

## THE SLEEPOVER

JOSH HAD BEEN LATE HOME FROM WORK, AND AS soon as he'd gotten in the door he headed straight for the shower to get cleaned up before Brian arrived. So he was still in the bathroom when I heard the loud, firm thuds of Brian knocking on the door. When I opened the door there was a fleeting flash of disappointment on Brian's face; he would have been expecting Josh. It was gone in an instant though, and he looked uninterested, even a little bored by the sight of me. "Hey," he said.

"Hey Brian, come in." I gestured and stepped out of his way so he could step inside, and I closed the door behind him. "Josh's still in the shower, he should be out any second. Can I get you a beer or something?"

"A beer would be good." He said it kind of dismissively, like he was giving an order to a waiter or something. He casually sauntered into the living room and sat down on the sofa.

I went into the kitchen and grabbed two beers out of the fridge. I popped the caps off as I walked back to the living room, and I handed one to Brian.

"How's your day been?" I asked him, somewhat awkwardly.

"Good." He didn't seem that interested in talking.

"I'm glad you could come back. Josh had fun last time. We both had fun."

He smirked. "I bet." He took a swig of his beer. "So did I. Your boyfriend takes dick like a pro."

I didn't know what to say to that. Fortunately Josh appeared just at that second, towel wrapped around his waist and hair still wet from the shower.

"Hey handsome," he said to Brian, grinning.

Brian stood up. "There's my boy." He stood, took two purposeful steps towards Josh, rested his one free hand on his waist, and kissed him. Josh seemed to melt into it, and as Brian slowly moved his hand around to his back Josh leaned back and let Brian kiss him with more force.

Brian whipped the towel away to reveal Josh's perfect bubble butt and his already hardening cock. He grabbed Josh's cock and balls in one hand tightly and asked "Did you miss me?"

"Yes," Josh replied, a little too emphatically.

Brian held out his beer in my direction. "Hold my beer," he ordered.

I quickly grabbed the half-empty bottle of beer, and Brian's free hand gripped Josh by the back of the neck as he kissed him again. It was astonishing to see Josh slip into such a trance each time Brian kissed him.

Brian pushed down on the back of Josh's head, and Josh quickly took the cue. He dropped to his knees, unbuckled Brian's belt and opened the fly of his jeans. I could see the outline of Brian's large cock starting to become erect, and James started to lick it through his underwear. "It smells so fucking good," he sighed. He burrowed in there, and started to pull down Brian's jeans a little to get at his balls. He licked them, and tried to get as much of them in his mouth as possible.

Josh looked up at Brian, right in his eyes, as he slowly peeled down his underwear. Brian's beast of a cock sprung out and bobbed around for a second or two. *Fuck, it's big.* I had forgotten just how big it was.

Josh wasted no time. He plunged the whole thing all the way down his throat until he gagged. He started to pull away but Brian rested a firm hand on the back of his head. He sputtered and gagged some more, but then regained his composure and went to work servicing that cock. Brian kept doing it like that, holding Josh's head in place with his cock deep down his throat, holding him there till he started to gag then releasing him with a gasp.

Josh always loved it when guys were a little rough with him when he was giving them head. I could never quite pull it off myself; it felt disrespectful, forced, awkward. But Brian was giving him what he needed.

Eventually Brian started to get rougher still, until he was holding Josh's head in place and fucking his face. Deep, and fast, and hard. Pulling out just long enough for Josh to gasp for breath before ramming it back in. It looked like more than I'd be able to handle, but Josh seemed to be loving every second of it.

After a few minutes Brian pulled his cock out one last time and stopped. Josh panted, gasping to get his breath back and wiping the saliva off his face.

"Bedroom. Now."

Josh sprung to his feet, took Brian by the hand and dragged him into the bedroom like an over-eager puppy on a walk. I followed, trying to stay silent and out of the way.

"Get on the bed. On your hands and knees."

Josh quickly obliged, getting on all fours facing away from Brian. I walked around them so I was watching Josh side-on.

This time it was Brian who dropped to his knees. He studied Josh's smooth, pink, freshly showered ass. He ran his hand across one of Josh's butt cheeks, appreciating the smooth skin. He touched Josh's hole lightly with the tips of three fingers, and Josh responded with a contented moan.

Brian leaned in. He kissed right on the crease where that firm bubble-butt met the top of Josh's toned, lean thigh. The he let his lips drag softly across his skin towards his hole.

Josh was letting out a quiet, subtle moan, and I could hear the quivering in his voice as he anticipated what was coming next. Brian pulled his mouth away, just for a second or two, to make Josh wait just a little bit longer. Then he extended his long, wide tongue and licked Josh's hole.

"God that's good," Josh groaned.

Brian licked all over Josh's hole, using the full surface of his tongue, like he was licking an ice cream cone. Getting the skin and the little trail of hair around Josh's hole sopping wet. Then with a hand on each butt cheek he spread the two of them further apart, forcing his tongue right into Josh's waiting hole. Josh let out a long, emphatic, "Yeaaahhh," and I could see his whole body shift position as it became visibly more relaxed.

They stayed like that, for a couple of minutes, Josh letting out little moans every time Brian got in deep with his tongue.

He stopped long enough to ask, "You like that?"

"It's incredible," Josh gushed.

He licked a little more, then asked, "You think you're ready for my cock now?"

Josh's reply was an almost inaudible whisper. "Yes please."

Brian stood up. He looked over at me for the first time in a while. "Lube."

I quickly ran over to the bedside table and grabbed the condom and lube I'd put out for them. I offered them up to Brian.

He looked at them. "This again." He looked annoyed, and a little bored.

When I said nothing, he said to me, "Don't you remember? I told your boyfriend here that next time I was gonna cum in his ass."

Fuck, the idea of that was so hot it made me want to blow right there and then. Part of me wished I could see Brian slide his bare cock into Josh, and see the moment he filled him. But rules were rules; Josh and I had talked about it and agreed that what was said last time was just dirty talk, heat of the moment stuff.

"We, we —" I was such a nervous wreck I couldn't barely get the words out. "We have a rule."

"You remember, don't you boy?" he asked, this time to Josh.

"Yeah," Josh replied, wistfully.

"That's what you want, isn't it? You wanna feel daddy's load inside you?"

"Fuck," Josh replied, the longing in his voice palpable. He paused for a few seconds. "That sounds so good."

"You want to feel my raw cock inside you?"

Josh paused again. "Yes." He turned and looked me in the eyes, his face painted with guilt.

Brian looked at me, with a cocky, faux-innocent look on his face. "Sounds like he doesn't want me to follow your rule."

I was floored. I wasn't sure what to say. Part of me was angry as hell, part of me was so horny I thought I might combust.

"I don't think you want me to follow it either." He looked deep into my eyes, staring me down. A challenge. "Do you?"

I looked at the condom in my hand. I looked at Josh staring at me, the guilt gone. Now he was just staring at me with pleading in his eyes. I thought about Brian's big cock releasing its seed inside Josh. If I was honest, that's the way I'd always pictured it happening when I'd thought about Brian coming back, even when Josh and I had agreed to keep on using protection.

"No," I admitted.

Brian smiled, triumphant. "Good cuck. I knew you wouldn't actually want to try restrict my guy from doing its thing."

I put the condom in my pocket, not sure what else to do with it. I looked at Josh; he looked relieved. He mouthed a silent "Thank you."

"You know what," Brian said, obviously enjoying humiliating me. "Since you're being so accommodating, I'll do you a solid. I'll let you lube me up."

I may have been half-expecting him to go raw, but I wasn't expecting that. I was a little stunned for a second; I looked down at his thick, hard cock. The thought of being able to touch it myself had never actually occurred to me until now.

I must have been standing there in stunned silence for a while, because eventually Brian prompted me: "So, are you gonna lube me up or not?"

I snapped out of it. "Yes! Yes. Thank you." I flicked the cap off the bottle and squeezed a generous amount of lube into the palm of my hand. I reached slowly for Brian's cock, then hesitated. Surely it was a joke. Surely he wouldn't let me touch it.

The two of them sniggered at my nervous hesitance, making me blush even more than I already was. I took a deep breath, and took his cock in my hand.

The instant I touched it my dick pulsed. I could feel my heartbeat pounding in my brain. Brian's cock was so hard, it was like it was skin over metal instead of skin over muscle. And so thick. For a second I didn't understand why it felt so different to holding my own, but then I realised: when I hold my own dick my thumb wraps around it and rests on my fingers, but with Brian's cock I couldn't even wrap my hand the whole way around it.

Studying his penis close-up for the first time, I slowly slid my hand up and down it, covering every inch of skin with a layer of lube. I realised I was going to need more lube.

I squeezed another palmful of lube into my hand and ran it over his cock, making sure I got plenty on the head so it would slide in nice and easy. I went carefully, like I was handling a valuable artifact, or a work of art. I *was* handling a work of art.

I ran my hand up and down his shaft one more time than was strictly necessary, then I reluctantly released it from my grip. I finally summoned up the will to look Brian in the face. He looked amused. Of course he did.

"Thank you, Simon," he said with mock sincerity. "Now sit the fuck down and get out of my way."

I did what I was told, sitting down on my stool. I watched as Brian lined his cockhead up against Josh's ass. "You ready, boy?" he asked.

"Yes!" Josh replied emphatically, impatiently. "Hurry up and fuck me."

Watching that huge, slick, bare cock start to enter Josh was probably the most erotic thing I'd ever seen in my life. The way it just slid smoothly in, skin on skin, all the way to the base.

"Holy fuck your ass feels amazing," Brian groaned.

I watched as he pulled it out slowly, then pushed it back in. I thought about the feeling of fucking Josh raw, a feeling that only I had experienced since the two of us first got together. I thought about that sensation, having a tight ass wrapped around your cock, nothing between the two to dull the feeling. And then I thought about how much tighter and firmer it must feel for a cock as thick as that.

*Fuck, no. I haven't even touched it yet.* I could feel the surge already though, the cum coursing through networks of my vas deferens and urethra towards the climax of erupting out of me. I wanted to stop it but it was far too late. I let out a sad little moan as the cum spilled out of my penis and into my underwear.

The two of them didn't stop fucking for a second, But Brian obviously noticed because he said to Josh, "Looks like your boyfriend just came in his pants." They both giggled at that. I felt ridiculous.

The next thirty minutes was agony, once that post-orgasm regret kicked in. I watched Brian Fuck Josh from behind, pin him down and fuck him into the mattress, roll him over and fuck him missionary, fuck him with his legs in the air. I had no idea how he managed to last that long, especially raw. I never could. It was much more passionate this time; they made out with each other constantly, with a sense of intimacy and longing for each other that I hadn't expected. Josh got on top of Brian and rode him, slamming his ass down on Brian's pelvis to take his cock as deep and hard as he possibly could, and wailing from the pleasure of it. He was possessed.

"Fuck, fuck, I'm so fucking close," Josh panted. "I don't want to cum yet. Not till you breed me."

Brian pushed him off and flipped him onto his front, face down on the bed. Now his head was facing me, but he didn't look up or even seem to realise I was still in the room. Brian lined his cock up and rammed it hard into Josh's ass. He lowered himself onto him, his chest against Josh's back and his hands holding up his weight like he was doing push-ups on top of him. In that position he rammed Josh's ass into the bed. Josh buried his face in the bedsheets and wailed as his ass got slammed.

"Fuck yeah. Fuck, it's coming. You ready for it?"

"Oh fuck, breed me. Fucking breed me!"

Suddenly Brian's whole body tensed, and with a howl he orgasmed hard.

"Oh god!" Josh whimpered.

"Fuck! Fuck! Fuck. Fuck." Brian's face clenched as tight as his body he continued to unload in Josh's ass.

That set Josh off too. I couldn't tell exactly what his dick was doing because it was buried in the bedsheets, but from the look on his face and the sound of his sob it sounded like he was cumming hard too.

Brian's orgasm finally subsided, and he collapsed on top of Josh. He kissed his ear, and his neck, and his cheek. Then he looked up at me with a satisfied, superior look in his eye.

They both looked exhausted. They lay there in silence, breath heaving, for several minutes. Then Brian slowly pulled out and rolled off. As he did, I got to see his cock, weighty and engorged and glistening with the cum he'd just put inside my fiancé.

Josh opened his eyes, and seemed to realise that I was still there. He looked at me sheepishly, and then pulled himself up. "Fuck, that was incredible," he said, more to Brian than for my benefit. The two of them kissed, standing there naked in front of me. "You must have cum fucking gallons inside me."

Brian laughed. "You're having my babies, for sure."

"Shower?"

Brian nodded. Without a word to me they left the room together.

I sat there in stunned silence for a few minutes, still not quite believing what I'd seen. I heard the shower start up, and their muffled voices.

I got up and crept towards the bed. I got in close, and homed in on the patch where Josh's ass had been when they finished. Right there in that spot the sheets were wet with two patches of semen. One big patch where Josh had cum with his cock pressed into the mattress. And another patch a few inches away, of semen that had leaked from Josh's ass. Semen that Brian had put in him.

Eventually the two of them came back into the room, still naked but now clean and with skin flushed pink from the heat of the shower. I was glad it was finally over, and I hoped that Brian would hurry up and get out of here faster than he had last time.

"Baby…" Josh said, in that voice he always used when he was about to ask me to do something I didn't want to. "Brian's going to stay the night. That's all good, right?"

My stomach sunk. I wasn't quite sure what to say. Although a second later my penis kicked into gear and twitched to let me know it maybe wasn't such a bad thing after all.

Before I could say anything, Brian threw me a pillow. Instinctively I caught it, although it took another second for me to comprehend why he'd passed it to me.

"Fuck off, dickhead. You're on the sofa."

# CHAPTER 4

## LOCKED OUT

I COULD TELL AS WE GOT CLOSER TO THE AIRPORT that Josh was getting more and more excited. In the short time since he'd met Brian he'd become much more into him than I'd seen him get with any of our other bulls. To be honest, it worried me a little. But at the same time I was happy for him. Plus I couldn't believe my luck getting to watch the two of them together.

In the two weeks since Brian had stayed over, he and Josh had been in regular contact: messaging, sending each other dirty pics, even the odd phone call or two. Then the other day Josh had asked me if I minded Brian forgoing his usual hotel room and staying over with us. "It seems kind of pointless for him to pay for a hotel, you know? He's only here for a night and I'm keen for him to stay over again, so it makes sense for him to just stay here the whole time."

My cock had jumped at the suggestion, so I'd told him without hesitating that I was ok with it. Now though, as I sat there behind the steering wheel on my way to pick him up from the airport, my nerves were all over the place and I wasn't questioning my decision.

"Babe, where will I sleep?" I asked. "Will I have to sleep on the sofa again?"

Josh thought about it for a second. "I guess," he replied. "I don't know. I guess we can sort it out when Brian's here. He might have a preference."

That moment last time, when they'd told me I wouldn't be sleeping with them, was so hot that I'd jerked off to it half a dozen times already in the last two weeks. And I had been insanely horny all night sleeping alone on that sofa, imagining them tangled in each others arms as they slept in their sweat and cum. But it was starting to dawn on me that if this was going to be the arrangement every fortnight from now on, I was going to be spending a lot of my time excluded from the action.

We didn't talk much as we got closer to the airport. I don't know if it was just our combined nerves and excitement that killed the conversation, or if it was the awkwardness of us both knowing that right now he wanted Brian much more than he wanted me. When we got to the airport I started to head to the parking area but Josh said, "You can just pull up in the pick-up zone if you want. I'll run in and get him."

I was disappointed. I wanted to see them meet, see how they reacted to each other when they saw each other again. But I switched lanes and drove up to the pick-up zone, and pulled over. The car was barely stopped when Josh opened the door and started to climb out. "Back in a minute, baby," he said. Then, like an afterthought, he leaned back in and gave me a kiss on the cheek before he jumped out of the car and closed the door.

He was barely in the airport door when I thought to myself, Fuck this. I want to see. I knew that if I left the car unattended there would be a good chance I'd end up with a parking ticket. And if I did, they'd both know I'd followed Josh in there. But in that moment the urge to see them overrode logic. So I jumped out of the car and ran into the airport after him.

It took me a second to get my bearings, but it was pretty easy to work out what gate Brian was arriving at. I ran towards it, but stopped close to the gate and hid behind a pillar once I saw Josh.

It only took a minute or two before passengers began spilling out through the arrival gate. Maybe twenty or so people came out before I caught sight of Brian, casually walking out with an overnight bag slung over his shoulder. As soon as he was clear of the crowd, Josh run over to him and threw his arms around him. Brian grabbed him in a tight embrace, and they kissed.

They turned to walk back, and for an instant I clocked the giddy, blissed out look on Josh's face before I snuck back behind the pillar and then darted off in the opposite direction so they wouldn't see me. As they headed towards the baggage claim I ran back to the car. I was relieved to find that there was no ticket on the windscreen. I hopped back into the driver's seat and waited.

After ten minutes or so I saw the two of them emerge through the sliding glass doors and make their way to the car. I hopped out, and stood awkwardly as I waited for them to get closer. When they were close enough I greeted Brian with a meek "Hi" and extended my hand to shake his.

"Hey," he replied. He took my hand and shook it. Hard. So hard it hurt. That had to be on purpose, just to show me who was in control.

I jumped back into the driver's seat. Brian opened the back door and climbed in. But to my surprise, instead of getting in the front with me, Josh climbed into the back seat with Brian. Instantly they were making out in the back seat, and Josh within a few seconds climbed onto Brian's lap.

We were barely through the ticket barrier when Josh

started to grapple with Brian's fly. I couldn't see down there in the rear view mirror, but I could tell by the moan of appreciation that Josh must have freed Brian's cock from his pants and was playing with it. By the time we got onto the motorway about a minute later, Josh was bent over in his seat taking Brian's cock in his mouth. I kept trying to sneak a look back there to see his mouth bobbing up and down on that big dick, but every time I did I started to veer out of my lane. So I tried my best to concentrate on the driving while listening to the slurping of Josh's messy blowjob as I drove.

The drive home seemed to last forever. The whole time, Josh had his mouth wrapped around Brian's cock, and Brian just sat back with his hands behind his head enjoying the ride.

When we finally pulled up outside our house, Brian shoved his meaty cock back into his pants, but didn't bother to do them up properly. We all hurriedly piled out of the car and headed up the short path to the house. As I fumbled with the keys, Brian pinned Josh up against the wall, grabbed him around the waist and kissed his neck. My eyes darted around as I frantically tried to get the key in the lock, making sure none of the neighbours were seeing the show.

As soon as I got the door unlocked I pushed it open, and they went in before me. They didn't break their embrace for a second. Brian gently pushed Josh down the hallway, guiding him by the waist. Josh just stumbled along backwards, leaning into Brian's kiss in a state of submissive lust. I followed slowly behind them, taking it all in. As they passed through the doorway into the bedroom, Brian shoved Josh down onto the bed. Then as he stepped towards him he slammed the door shut behind him, right in my face.

I stood there for a moment, stunned. *Was that on purpose? Surely they didn't mean to shut me out? Not yet, not until it was time to go to sleep.* For a few seconds I had no idea what to do. Then I knocked, gingerly.

"Fuck off!"

*Motherfucker.* This time I knocked harder. "Hey! I thought I was going to get to watch!" I wanted that to come out sounding tough, angry. But when I heard the words come out of my mouth it sounded more like pleading.

There was silence for a second. Then the door swung open abruptly and Brian was standing there. He looked pissed. "I told you to fuck off," he growled.

I started to stammer: "But—"

"Look, it's been two weeks and I want a bit of alone time with my boy. I might let you watch later. *If* you stop moaning like a little bitch and give us some peace."

I looked past him to where Josh was lying on the bed, already stripped down to his jocks with a massive boner. He just kind of shrugged. "Sorry baby. Maybe in a bit?"

With that Brian slammed the door in my face again. Seconds later I heard his low growls, combined with Josh's moans.

I was furious. For a moment I thought about barging in there. But instead I reached down and pulled out my already hard cock, and started jerking it.

I must have stood out there for forty-five minutes or more, trying to picture what they were doing inside my bedroom. At first, the low moans told me that they were probably undressing each other slowly, making out, exploring each other's cocks with their hands and their mouths. But after a while I heard the unmistakeable sound of Josh crying out with pain and pleasure as Brian entered him, and before long I started to hear the bed creak and the headboard hit the wall as Brian started fucking him with more and more intensity.

Soon Josh was wailing with delight and the bed was thumping and creaking like it was being thrown around the room. The sounds were muffled, but every now and then I could make out particular words. "So deep.... Fuck me.... I love it..." And I heard the slap as Brian spanked Josh's ass. When I heard him say "Please... give me your load," I couldn't contain myself anymore. I shot a massive load that landed all over the door and the hallway floor. I slowly slunk to the floor, expecting to hear the sound of Brian orgasming and breeding my boyfriend. But they kept going. On, and on.

I must have sat there for another twenty minutes before I heard the pace suddenly pick up, the bed banging so hard and so fast against the wall that it was making the floor I was sitting on vibrate. I heard Josh beg, and then I heard what could only be described as a roar as Brian busted his nut in Josh's ass.

After that there was silence, apart from the occasional murmur that I couldn't make out. I wondered what they were talking about in there, if the subject of their conversation had turned to me at all.

Eventually I decided I should get up and make some dinner. I walked into the kitchen, and found a bunch of ready-made stuff that I could cook up quickly. I was a nervous wreck, in no state to try and cook properly. And besides, I wanted to be done quickly in case they started fucking again and I wanted to go listen.

After a little while I heard the door open, and a few seconds later Josh came into the kitchen. He was in his jocks, his hair all over the place and his skin still shiny with sweat.

"Hey," he said, apologetically. "Are you okay?"

"Yeah," I replied, nodding. I didn't know if it was true or not but it seemed like a good enough answer for now.

"Sorry he kicked you out. I didn't know he was going to do that."

"You didn't seem too bothered by it though, right?" I let that sound more wounded than I'd meant to.

Josh's expression changed from concerned to defensive.

"I'm sorry" I said quickly. "I don't know why I said that.

Honestly it's fine. It was really hot, listening to you guys but not being able to see what you were doing."

"You listened?" That made him smile.

"Of course I listened. It sounded like you were really enjoying yourself."

With that, Josh grinned from ear to ear. "Fuck yeah, it was unbelievable. He fucks like a god."

My still-limp cock twitched a little hearing that. It was already obvious I could never measure up to Brian, but it also felt incredibly hot to be told how good he was by my fiancé.

I changed the subject. "Hey, I made you guys dinner. It's almost ready."

"Thanks, baby." Josh kissed me. When he did I could taste dick on his breath.

I started dishing up the food, and a minute or so later Brian sauntered into the room, buck naked, his huge cock swaying from side to side as he walked. He stood behind Josh, put his arms around him and pulled him in, so that Josh's ass was pressed up against his cock. He kissed the back of his neck.

"Simon made us dinner, daddy," Josh told him.

"Cool." He looked at me. "When you're done dishing that up can you clean up the puddle of cum you left on the floor in the hallway."

That made Josh chuckle.

I handed them their dinner, and they wandered out into the living room. Before I joined them, I quickly grabbed a cloth and went out into the hallway to wipe up the cum from the floor and the bedroom door, then I grabbed my food and joined them at the dining table.

As they ate they casually chatted; it was kind of surreal, because they talked about normal stuff like their jobs and their gym routines, as if they were just friends. As if they hadn't been fucking fifteen minutes ago while I sat outside listening to them. I noticed though, as the conversation went on, that not much of it was directed at me.

After dinner, Josh got up and started clearing the plates. As he did, Brian gave him a hard slap on the ass and said, "Let the cuck do that. You're joining me in the bedroom."

"Definitely," Josh replied with a grin as he dropped the plates back down on the table.

Brian looked at me as he stood up. "Guess you can join us this time, cuck. Just keep quiet, okay."

Josh followed Brian to the bedroom. I hurriedly took the plates out to the kitchen and dumped them on the bench, and made a beeline for the bedroom.

When I came in Brian was laid out on the bed, his arms stretched behind his head. Josh was just starting to climb on top of Brian, positioning his ass on Brian's crotch. I sat down in my chair in the corner.

"You fucked me so good before," Josh said to Brian in a quiet voice.

"Glad you liked it," Brian replied. He pulled Josh in, so he was lying with his chest resting on his. Then he kissed him, slowly and gently. "There's plenty more where that came from."

"I wish you were here to fuck me every day. When you're not here, I think about you fucking me all the time. I think about your arms pinning me down, your cock stretching me out. Honestly, no one has ever fucked me the way you have before."

Brian let out a deep, gravelly chuckle. "Why, have all your boyfriends been useless like this one?" He looked over at me and grinned as he said it.

"Some of them have been more hung," Josh said. "And most of them have fucked me better than Simon. But still nothing compared to you, daddy. When you're inside me it makes me feel complete, and when you take your cock out of me I feel empty again. I don't know what it is, it's like nothing I've experienced before."

With that, they kissed again. They made out slowly, with a kind of tenderness that I had never seen Josh exhibit with anyone else, even me if I was totally honest. They just lay there, kissing each other and touching every part of each other for what seemed like forever. After a while Brian started to thrust slowly against Josh, rubbing the tip of his cock against Josh's hole. He lined up his hard cock against Josh's hole, and Josh pushed down onto it. It slid in easily, loosened from earlier in the evening.

Then they slowly fucked, Josh writhing his ass up and down, milking Brian's cock with it. They made love for well over an hour at the same, slow speed, Josh's whimpers muffled by Brian's mouth as they kissed. They whispered to each other, too quietly for me to hear what they were saying. The whole time, I didn't see Josh touch his own cock at all, but it was rock hard. As was mine.

Eventually I pulled out my phone and checked the time. It was late, and I had to work in the morning. I didn't want to leave this, but I figured maybe I should. Even though Brian was inside Josh, it was like they weren't even fucking anymore, just two bodies joined from both the inside and the outside. And I felt like I was intruding on their enjoyment of each other.

So I stood up. "Guys, I'm going to bed," I announced. "I'm guessing you probably want me to sleep on the sofa anyway, so..."

Neither of them seemed to hear; they didn't say a word or even look in my direction. So I walked out of the room and pulled the door almost, but not completely, closed behind me. I grabbed some blankets and a pillow, and crashed out on the sofa.

I woke up in the middle of the night to the dull thud of

the headboard hitting the wall, and Josh's gasps. I had no idea what time it was, and I quickly drifted back to sleep, my hand holding my hard cock.

———

When I woke up in the morning, the first thing I did was make coffee. Then, holding two cups carefully in my hands, I knocked softly on the bedroom door. I heard a half grunt, half "yeah", so I pushed the door open and went in.

Brian and Josh were tangled together, Josh's head resting on Brian's chest. The sheets were half pulled down so I could admire both of their muscular torsos as they lay there. The room stank of sex and sweat, and it made me instantly horny. Both of them were dozily coming to life.

I put a coffee on each of the bedside tables. "How are you guys this morning?" I asked.

"Good thanks, baby," Josh replied. "Thanks for the coffee."

"No problem," I assured him. "Hey I have to go to work real soon, I'm already late. But Brian, I wanted to check whether you wanted a lift to the airport tonight."

Josh looked at Brian awkwardly, then at me. "Didn't I tell you, baby? Brian booked his flight for Sunday so he can stay an extra couple of days. Sorry... I totally thought I told you that already."

"Staying till Sunday? You mean here with us?"

"Yeah," Brian replied sleepily. "I've still got a lot of stuff I want to do with my boy here." As he said the words '*my boy*' he put his arms around Josh and gave him a long, lazy kiss.

"Hope that's all good baby?" Josh asked hopefully.

"He'll be fine," Brian assured him. Then he looked straight at me. "He likes sleeping on the sofa."

# CHAPTER 5

## LOCKED UP

JOSH AND BRIAN DID THEIR USUAL THING ON THE way home from the airport: Josh was all over Brian's cock in the back seat of the car. We got a few mortified looks from people in cars along the motorway, and while I was embarrassed and humiliated by it, Josh and Brian didn't seem to notice.

When we got home though, they didn't head straight for the bedroom. Instead Brian put down his bags in the hallway and turned to me. "Hey Simon, I have something for you."

*He never calls me Simon. It's always "cuck".*

"For me?"

Brian fished around in his bag, pulled out a small box, and handed it over. Josh obviously wasn't in on the surprise, because he looked just as interested as me to find out what was inside.

"Thanks, Brian," I said, my suspicions aroused.

I carefully opened the box. Inside a was a small velvet pouch, so I took it out, untied the string and put my hand in. It felt like there were several pieces, none of which I recognised by shape, so I gently poured the contents out onto the dining room table. Although I'd never seen one exactly like it, I knew what it was the moment the metal pieces fell out of the bag. The ring. The bar. The short, curved, phallic-shaped metal dome. The padlock. "A cock cage?"

"You're welcome," Brian said with a smug grin.

"Oh, thanks," I said, a little confused.

The confusion must have been obvious to him. "You want to know why I got it for you." It was more of a statement than a question.

"Sure."

"Well, a couple of reasons. For one thing, Josh told me about how you wanted to fuck him the other day. I can't have that, you know?"

"What do you—"

"He's my boy. I fuck him, and I decide who else fucks him. And *you're* not fucking him. If you're caged, it's clear to you not to bother trying."

"Hun...?" I looked at Josh, pleading. The look I got back from him was slightly apologetic, but mostly impassive.

"And the other reason: I'm okay with you watching occasionally. But when you jerk that baby dick it's distracting and, to be honest, kinda pitiful. So I figured the cage would help with that, so you don't feel the urge to stroke it when we let you watch."

*Fuck this. He has got to be fucking kidding.*

"Josh, I need to talk to you about this." I did my best attempt at sounding firm. "Alone."

Brian smirked, but shrugged as if to say *'okay, sure'*. He wandered off into the kitchen.

"Josh," I said, "I think this is going too far. I'm down with him humiliating me, kicking me out of my own bedroom, making me drive him around and cook him fucking dinner. That's all fine. But surely he's not suggesting that I can't even fuck you anymore! And surely you don't want that, do you?"

Josh looked at the ground, then up at the ceiling. "I dunno, baby." He thought about it for a second."I don't want you to do anything you don't want to do. Nothing that doesn't turn you on. But I kinda figured this would turn you on. Doesn't it?"

"No!" I lied. "Yes. Maybe. Okay, yes, it turns me on heaps. But it's a little extreme, isn't it? You're my fiancé. I want to be able to fuck you sometimes. Or even jerk off, for that matter."

At that moment Brian came back in.

"Hey Brian, we're not quite done yet," I told him, trying to sound stern but still not quite pulling it off.

"I heard you from out there, I thought maybe this would help." He pulled out his phone. "You don't want to be caged because you want to still be able to fuck my boy. Because you think my boy wants you fucking him. He's a nice guy so he'd never say it to you himself, but take a look."

He handed me his phone, open to a chat. I looked closer; it was a chat between him and Josh.

> **J** — He was trying to fuck me but you've wrecked me so much I don't even feel him anymore lol

> What made you want to get fucked by the cuck?

> He was desperate for it

> **J** — Kept sulking till I let him

> I don't like him fucking you. You're my boy, you know that, right?

Fuck it's hot hearing you say that

Yeah I know. I don't want
him to fuck me either

I was thinking of you the whole time,
wishing it was your big dick inside me

Sounds like I need to
do something about it

Haha you gonna tell him he's not
allowed to fuck me anymore?
Make me all yours?

I looked at Josh. "You don't want to have sex with me anymore?"

"Shit," Josh looked a little panicked. "Brian, I didn't think you were gonna show him that stuff."

"Josh?"

He looked me straight in the eyes. "I love you, you know that, right? That hasn't changed. I'm marrying you! But Brian fucks me like no one ever has. And when you try fuck me, it's just not the same."

Even though I knew that already, it still stung a little.

"I've seen the porn and the blogs you follow, I know you get off on this kind of stuff. This could be good for both of us. You get cucked properly, like the most extreme version of your fantasy. And I get fucked the best I ever have been." He paused to test my reaction, but I didn't react, I was too confused. So he continued: "Hey, these things are always evolving. Maybe you could try it out for a bit and see how it goes."

I looked at Brian. I could see a hint of a smirk. I looked at the cage. I thought about it, locked on my dick, locking it away where I couldn't use it or touch it. I thought about what I'd just seen on Brian's phone, the fact that my fiancé didn't want me to have sex with him anymore. It was sad, but it sent those usual pulses of electricity through my groin. The ones that told me I was into it.

I sighed. "Okay."

"Baby that's great!" Josh kissed me. "Are you going to put it on now?"

"I guess," I replied. I picked it up and studied it, working out how the different components fit together. "I'll go put it on."

"Why don't you put it on right here?" asked Brian.

*Shit. He really wants to make this as humiliating as possible.* "Okay," I said.

I dropped my trousers and my underwear. Surprisingly, my cock was still soft despite the way I was being humiliated in front of the two of them. I put the ring around my scrotum; it was cold. I attached the bar that held the ring together, which was also what the cage would attach to. I slid the cold, metal cage over my cock, and fit it to the bar.

"It's not too big, is it?" asked Brian. "I bought a small one." Both he and Josh sniggered at that, but Josh quickly stopped himself and tried to look serious.

"It fits," I replied.

Brian picked up the tiny padlock from the table and handed it to me. "Time to lock up."

I took the padlock from his hand. I looked at Josh, gave him a few seconds to speak up, just in case he was going to change his mind, or in case he was going to reveal that this was just a joke. Maybe it was; maybe after they'd finished fucking they'd tell me they were just messing with me to step up the cuckold fantasy, and I could take it off. I slid the lock through the hole, and snapped it shut. I took the key out, and then asked "So what should I do with the key?"

"I'll take that," Brian replied. He took the key from my hand, and then he reached into his pocket and pulled out a length of twine. He slid the key onto the twine, then tied the twine around his neck like a necklace. "This is where the key will live from now on," he told me. "So you know who's in charge."

With that my cock started to swell, which made the cage jerk suddenly. They both saw it, and it made them both laugh. "He likes it already," Brian said to Josh, gesturing at it.

"Baby, it's great," Josh said to me.

"Now," said Brian, "I've waited long enough to fuck my boy. Cuck, you can watch this time if you want."

We all headed to the bedroom. I sat on my familiar stool in the corner, my cock already starting to fill up the confines of the cage. Josh and Brian started to make out on the bed and strip each other's clothes off. Before long they were both naked and hard, Brian on top of Josh pinning him down on the bed and teasing his hole with his cock.

Josh grabbed the lube from the bedside table. "How do you want me, daddy?"

"On all fours," he ordered. "Facing the cuck."

Josh obediently got into position, and Brian lubed up his cock. He lined up behind Josh, also facing me. Then, looking straight into my eyes he slowly entered Josh from behind. Josh let out a blissful moan and closed his eyes in ecstasy as Brian's cock filled him.

My cock now reached the limits of how much it could swell in its new cage. As they started to fuck I felt my cock straining against the firm metal of the cage, and it hurt.

Brian's fucking quickly got more intense. He was still wearing the key to my cage on the string around his neck, and it swung back and forth with each thrust into Josh's ass. For a while they both forgot I was there, but then Brian looked at me and smiled. "Hey cuck, you enjoying this?"

"Yes."

"Is it making you hard?" He laughed.

He leaned down, till his face was right by Josh's ear. He thrust hard into him, and Josh cried out. "Baby, do you like me fucking you?"

"Yes daddy! I fucking love it!"

"Who's cock do you want?"

"Yours, daddy. Yours is the only cock I want."

"Are you glad you never have to get fucked by that little cuck dick again?"

"Yes!"

"You belong to me now, right boy?"

"Yes! I'm yours. Please, just never stop fucking me!"

At that, my cock strained so hard in its cage that I cried out in pain.

Brian looked at me and grinned. "Does that hurt, cuck? Better get used to it, because you're gonna be watching us fuck all night."

He wasn't wrong, either. They fucked for literally hours, and I sat there the whole time, in agony as my cock tried to expand farther than the cage would let it. I think it was after two in the morning when Brian finally unloaded in Josh's ass, and told me "Get the fuck out." By then my cock was so sore I could have sworn it was bleeding if I couldn't see for myself. Usually I was disappointed when I got kicked out for the night, but this time around the pain had exhausted me so much I was relieved. I stumbled out of the room, collapsed onto the sofa, and fell asleep.

# CHAPTER 6

## THE BEST MAN

IT WAS A TUESDAY NIGHT, AND WE'D BOTH FINISHED work at a reasonable time which meant we had a bit of time on our hands. Being mid-week it also meant Josh and I had the place to ourselves, with no sign of Brian to distract Josh from the task at hand. So we decided to do some wedding planning; Josh ordered takeout, while I made a jug full of margaritas. Then we parked ourselves at the dining table, surrounded by lists and laptops and samples.

We'd already decided on a venue, and booked it months ago. Nine Mile Bay was a small resort about four hours south of the city. It was ideal: warm, secluded, with a sandy beach and calm water for swimming. The resort would have other people there at the same time, but there was a large section fairly separate from the rest of the accommodation where the guests could stay and the reception could be held. It was close enough that our friends and family could enjoy a weekend out of the city without having to travel too far.

It was hard to get a booking for a wedding there, which is why we had picked a date fast and booked it. The date we'd picked was approaching fast though, and we needed to get on with it if we were going to get everything organised on time. We only had three months left, and there was so much to arrange. I'd always known wedding planning was intense, but I had no idea how many details there were.

And it hadn't helped that the task hadn't had Josh's full attention lately, either. For the month or so since I'd gotten my cage, Brian had been in town for work at least a couple of nights each week, which meant those nights were a write-off when it came to wedding planning. They'd been fucking hot though; some nights I'd get to watch, sitting there leaking in my cage while the two of them fucked like rabbits. Other nights I wasn't allowed to, so instead I'd sit in the next room listening to them fuck and concentrating on the feeling of my swollen cock pressing painfully against the metal of my cage.

But then we'd got the news: Brian was getting a promotion as part of a restructuring at his work, and the new job meant no more regular travelling between cities. His visits weren't over just yet, because the restructure wasn't taking effect for another three months yet — right around the time of our wedding, give or take — but it was clear that he and Josh now had a time limit on their relationship.

Josh had taken it hard. He'd been brooding for a couple of weeks now, and he'd been particularly critical whenever I did anything wrong. In fact the level of emotion he'd reacted with when he found out had been kind of troubling, and to be honest it made me relieved that their relationship was coming to an end. It had been beyond hot, but I could see that it was maybe getting a little out of hand. So I felt that ultimately this was probably for the best.

It was kind of perfect, really: we'd have a fresh start together, as a married couple, just as Josh's relationship with Brian came to a natural conclusion. I wasn't about to say that to Josh though, not while he was still sulking like a surly teenager.

So between Josh's desperation to spend as much time with Brian whenever he was here, and his sulkiness whenever Brian was away, we hadn't found much time to do anything together, especially not wedding planning. These last few days though I felt like Josh had turned a corner, and I was determined to re-inject a bit of positivity into the whole process. Hence the big jug of margaritas to drink while we powered through the planning.

As we worked through the guest list, I asked Josh "So, are you going to ask Rico to be your best man?"

Josh shook his head. "Nope. I want to find him something good to do though."

"I always figured he'd be your best man. You guys have known each other since you were kids."

Josh said nothing.

"So... who, then?"

Josh looked a little nervous, and took a second before he said anything. In that second I already knew what he was going to say: "I was kind of thinking I might ask Brian to do it."

That made me feel slightly sick in my stomach, but slightly turned on at the same time. "Whoa." I wasn't sure exactly what to say. "You barely know him. To be honest it hadn't even occurred to me to invite him to the wedding." Other than in my fantasies where I watched them fuck in their tuxes right before the wedding ceremony, but I didn't want to admit to that right now.

"Yeah. I guess I just thought it would be cool to have him there. I thought about just asking Rico, but when I pictured it in my mind Brian just seemed like the natural choice."

"Okay..."

"I mean, he's the obvious choice for best man. He's the best man I've ever had."

There was silence for a second as that sunk in, before Josh nervously corrected himself: "Apart from you, baby, you know."

I sat there for a second, trying to get my bead around it. *This is so fucked up*, I thought. Obviously I was right into getting cuckolded, and being cuckolded at your own wedding is the height of the fantasy. I'd jerked off to that fantasy count-less times in the past, back when marriage was just a distant possibility. But surely it was taking it a step too far to actually have your bull as your husband's best man?

I tried to picture myself standing there, looking Josh in the eyes as we each said our wedding vows, with Brian right there with that smug smirk on in front of all of our wedding guests. Knowing that even though Josh was marrying me, he would have probably been fucked by another man hours before the wedding. Knowing that he could stand there saying wedding vows to me, with Brian's seed still inside him. Would Josh even be thinking about me when he married me? Or would he be in a state of slut lust, counting down the minutes till the next time Brian fucked him.

"Babe," Josh asked. "Are you okay with it?"

I honestly didn't know. On one hand everything about it screamed red flags. We barely even knew Brian, and Josh was contemplating sidelining his best friend to give him the best man position. But on the other hand it seemed unbelievably hot, the idea of having Josh's bull there at our wedding. And it would be a perfect way to end our arrangement with him on a high. I realised that my cock was straining in its cage at the thought of it. *I guess that settles it.* "Yeah. I'm okay with it. If you want Brian you should have Brian."

Josh beamed. "Thanks baby. You're the best. I love you so much, and I can't believe I get to marry you in three months time."

"Have you already asked him about it?" I asked.

"No, I wanted to wait till I'd checked it with you. I'll call him right now." Never mind that we were in the middle of wedding planning and still had a bunch of other stuff to go through, Josh had obviously forgotten all about that in the rush of finding out he'd get to have Brian with him on our wedding day. He called Brian's number and tapped his fingers impatiently on the table as he waited for him to answer.

"Hey, daddy," he said when Brian finally answered. "How's things?"

I couldn't hear what Brian was saying on the other end, but it got Josh going.

"Me too. I've missed your cock so much."

"Fuck, I can't wait. That sounds so good. You gotta make sure you save a real big load for me, okay?"

"We're doing wedding planning. That's why I called. I wanted to wait and ask you in person, but I was too excited so I'm just gonna do it now." He took a deep breath. "Will you be my best man?"

He obviously got the answer he wanted, because he started beaming from ear to ear. He covered the phone and whispered to me, "He said yes!"

Whatever Brian said next, it made him laugh. "Of course you can, daddy. Whatever you want."

"Ummm, I'll have to check but I'm sure Simon will be all good with that."

I tried to catch his eye to see what it was Brian was asking him, but Josh didn't seem to notice I was there and just carried on talking.

"Yeah, I guess you will. That'll be cool."

"Fuck, that sounds so hot. Fuck, you're getting me so hard right now."

"Yeah? You want that? Ok. Hang up and call me back by video, okay?" He got up and wandered out of the room without a word to me.

I debated whether I should go stand outside the door and listen while they had cam sex. But I figured there was too much work to do, so I got back to planning seating arrangements. I figured I should probably just give them a bit of privacy to celebrate the good news.

# CHAPTER 7

## OUTED

I WAS UP EARLY AFTER A NIGHT ON THE SOFA. BRIAN staying over for the whole weekend had become more or less a regular thing now, and I was starting to establish my own Saturday morning routine. I always got up early now, woken by the painful feeling of my morning erection straining against the confines of my cage. And when Brian was over I'd have to get up straight away and get stuck straight into a bunch of chores, because it was the only way I could take my mind off how much I wanted to touch my dick as soon as I thought about the two of them sleeping in my bed together.

I knew they'd sleep in later than me, and would fuck once they woke up, so I usually had a decent amount of time to myself. This morning I'd put on some laundry, watered the garden, and checked some emails. I'd also sorted through a box or two of junk from the shed out the back, which is something Josh and I had been slowly working through for a couple of months now whenever we got around to it. I was getting hungry so was keen to start making breakfast — I always cooked a big breakfast on a Saturday morning when Brian was in town, because I knew they'd both be hungry — but there was no point starting yet because I'd heard no signs of life, and I knew not to start cooking till they'd been fucking at least half an hour.

I'd just put the kettle on to make a second cup of coffee, when I heard a knock at the door. I opened it to find my brother, Ben, standing on the doorstep.

"Ben! This is a surprise. I didn't know you even got out of bed this early."

"Shows what you know, Si" he replied. "I've already been out for a run before I came here. Can I come in?"

My mind flashed instantly to the thought of Josh and Brian and what they'd soon be up to. "Umm, it's kind of not a great time right now to be honest. Could we maybe—"

"It's important, Si. It won't take long. What, are you like, cooking meth in there or something?"

*Fuck.* "No, it's fine, come in."

He walked straight into the kitchen, where the kettle was just coming to a boil. "Looks like I came right on time. Pour me a coffee, would you?"

I started making coffee. "What's up, Ben? What's this important thing you wanted to talk to me about?"

"Efficient, getting right into it. I like that, Si."

"What is it?" I asked, the frustration showing in my voice. I needed him to hurry the hell up so I could get him out of my house.

"Okay, so I guess it's not that important really," he admitted. "It's just our parents driving me nuts about wedding presents for you, and I just don't know what to tell them."

I sighed. "What do you mean?

"It's just Dad and Greta are obsessed with getting you the perfect wedding gift, but they don't know what to get and they don't want to ask you to ruin the surprise."

"Uh-huh."

"And then mum is obsessed with outdoing Dad, even

though she barely has the cash to get to the wedding in the first place, let alone get you something good."

"Uh-huh. So what I am I supposed to do?" I asked, pouring coffee. "And if they're all trying to surprise me why are you even telling me?" I handed Ben a cup of coffee.

"Thanks bro. Hey, where's the wife?"

"He's still in bed." *Hopefully still asleep for a while yet.*

Ben wandered out of the kitchen and into the living room, where he stopped. "Ah, I see why it isn't a good time," he said. As I caught up I saw that the blanket and pillow were still on the sofa from where I slept last night. "Trouble in gay paradise?"

"No, no, nothing like that. We just had a friend over." Not a lie; I am a terrible liar so if I can bend the truth a little bit the result is always better.

"Ah, ok. Cool," Ben said, pushing the blanket out of the way and sitting down on the sofa. "Well anyway, I just figured you could give me some clues, on the down-low, so I can tell them all what to get you. You know, to maintain the illusion that it's all still a surprise."

At that moment I heard something through the wall. A murmur, or a movement. One of them was awake.

"Okay, whatever. I'll think about it and get back to you." I needed him to leave, like, now.

I heard the bed creak.

"Okay. I mean, nothing springs to mind right now?"

The bed creaked again, and I heard what sounded like a moan.

*Fuck. They're going at it.*

"No. I'll email you. Later. Tomorrow." I was starting to panic. "Listen, I have a pretty busy day, and—"

"I've only just started my coffee, Si. Chill out, dude."

The bed creaked, and I heard some definite moaning. I was amazed Ben hadn't noticed it. I could feel myself start to go red with embarrassment. Even though he hadn't noticed anything yet, I was certain I was about to be outed as a cuck in front of my own brother. *Fuck. I need to get him out of here.* "Lets go out for coffee. Better coffee. And breakfast. You want breakfast?"

That's when it started. The bed started to creak and thud rhythmically against the wall, and Josh's moans picked up pace in time with the bed moving.

Ben looked up. "Fuck, what's he doing in there?"

*Shit.*

"Umm—"

"Fuck!" I heard Josh cry out, loud enough that the word was clear through the wall. "Harder!" Then the bed started pounding against the wall.

Ben looked confused. I could see it ticking over in his brain. I could almost see every individual realisation sink in: that was our bedroom through the wall, and I'd already said that Josh was still in there. I saw him look over at the blanket and the pillow on the sofa as he put it together in his head.

"Hey, I should probably go," he said, quickly getting up and scanning the room for somewhere to put his coffee down.

"Ummm it's not—" *It's not what it looks like? It's exactly what it looks like.*

I took the coffee cup from him, and Ben made a beeline for the front door. I followed him. "Hey, I'll email you wedding present ideas, okay?"

"Yup, sure." He looked so fucking awkward.

As we got into the hallway the noise stopped abruptly. And as I pulled the front door open for Ben to leave, the bedroom door opened too. It was like time stood still, as my brother and I stood there staring at the bedroom door as it swung open, and out stepped Brian. He was naked, his cock still half erect. He looked over at the two of us, gave us a nod, and said "Hey". Then he casually walked to the bathroom, and without even shutting the door, started taking a piss.

We both just stood there for a second, before Ben shook himself out of his stunned state and backed out the door. "Hey well, I'll see you later."

"Hey, wait!" I stepped outside after him, and pulled the door shut behind me. "Fuck, sorry about that."

"Hey don't worry about it," Ben replied in an attempt at nonchalance that was not at all convincing. "Each to their own, and all that. I'm sorry I barged in, I mean, you told me it wasn't a good time."

"Sorry."

Ben paused, tentatively. "Is everything all right, though?"

"Yes. Definitely. Its... I guess you probably wouldn't understand."

"All good. Not for me to judge, bro."

"Thanks."

He paused again, as if debating the wisdom of what he was about to say. "Jesus, that guy is *hung*." Then, with a slightly sheepish look on his face, he headed for the gate. "Later bro," he called out.

As soon as he was through the gate, he bolted. I turned to go back inside, but realised I'd just locked myself out. I banged on the door. "Josh! Guys!"

There was no answer. I was going to be out here for a while.

## Chapter 8

### The Bachelor Party

I stepped out onto the paving, two cocktails in hand. The cloudless sky was a vivid shade of blue, almost the same colour as the swimming pool. We'd gotten pretty lucky with our choice of days for our bachelor party.

We'd arrived at Nine Mile Bay earlier that morning, just the two of us. Most of the guests — relatives, workmates — wouldn't be arriving till the following day, but a few of our closest friends were coming over today for the party.

One of the good things about a same sex wedding is that you get to make up a whole lot of the traditions yourself. So we'd decided that instead of having separate bachelor parties we'd share one, and we'd organise it ourselves rather than leaving it up to the whims of our friends. No bar, no seedy strip club. Just us grooms and our closest friends, spending an afternoon chilling out in the pool with cocktails. Followed by an evening of getting messed up. Then tomorrow we could sleep off our hangovers all morning, meet the relatives when they turned up later in the day, and be ready to go for the wedding day itself the day after that.

Our room was amazing; it was almost a entire house. It

only had one bedroom, but it had a sizeable living area that opened out onto a private courtyard with its own small swimming pool. It was a shame we only had it for tonight, for the party. Tomorrow we'd be sleeping in separate rooms in the main hotel complex, and then after the wedding we'd have a hut down by the beach to ourselves.

By now most of the people had arrived. Josh, Hamish and Jonny were splashing around in the pool while the others lounged around sipping drinks and talking among themselves. I had a momentary feeling of self-consciousness as I surveyed their bodies. Apart from Ben — obviously the only straight guy in the room with his long board shorts — the other guys all had on swim briefs or short trunks, all tight enough to show off great asses and bulges that were obviously bigger than mine. I suddenly regretted wearing the tight, short little trunks I had on. I'd wanted to make the most of being allowed out of my cage for the time we were at the resort — Josh had told me when we arrived that I was allowed out until the wedding — and at the time I'd imagined myself looking sexy wearing little-to-nothing. But of course my attempts to get ripped for my wedding day hadn't gone quite as successfully as I'd imagined. Still, I reminded myself of the fact that they were all here to celebrate how I was about to marry the hottest piece of ass any of these guys have ever met. So even if I wasn't the best looking guy at the party, I was definitely the luckiest.

I handed Anthony and Hassan their cocktails and headed back into the kitchen to make one for myself. As I stepped back inside, out of the sun, I wondered for a moment how I ended up being the one serving the drinks at my own bachelor party. I guess I was the host though.

Before I reached the kitchen I heard a knock on the door. I made a beeline towards it, the butterflies in my stomach starting up again; there were only two or three people left to arrive, and one of them made me extremely nervous.

I opened the door, and it was Brian. He was wearing a muscle shirt that showed off his considerably muscular shoulders, and shorts that were just tight enough for his massive package to be obvious.

"Hey cuck," he said with a grin. "Happy bachelor party."

I tried feebly to act welcoming and nonchalant, even though my heart was racing already. Josh had told me that he'd instructed Brian to be on his best behaviour, and besides, half of the guys there already knew about him anyway. Still, the anticipation of what he might do, how much he might give away, how much he might humiliate me in front of my friends, terrified me. "Thanks Brian. Come on in. Can I get you a drink?"

He shut the door behind him. "Sure, what have you got?"

I motioned to the bench full of alcohol bottles. "Pretty much everything, I think."

"Surprise me," he said. Then, leaving me to make his drink, he wandered out to the pool. As I hurriedly stirred, I heard a ripple of greetings coming from outside. I hurried out into the courtyard just in time to see Josh pulling himself out of the pool. "Hey daddy, glad you could make it," he said, wrapping his arms around him and planting a long, passionate kiss on his lips. Brian grabbed onto Josh's ass in his skimpy briefs.

With that a few of the guests let out a cheer. I scanned the scene: a few of them were laughing, enjoying the show. Jonny looked a little confused, but he had a bit of an idea what our relationship was like so he didn't seem to bothered. A couple of them — Ben and Hamish in particular — looked a little concerned.

They broke their kiss, finally. "So," Brian said to Josh, "Last night of partying as a single man. You gonna make the most of it?"

"Oh yeah, of course!" Josh replied. "I'm ready for

anything." With that he jumped into the pool. Brian pulled off his singlet, and then his shorts, revealing an even tighter pair of swimming trunks that looked like they were struggling to contain his monster cock. Then he jumped in after Josh. I put his drink down on a table by the pool and walked over to where the others were chatting, trying to pretend like the situation was normal.

"Hey Si," said Rico. "I can see why Josh goes for that guy. He looks like he must be hung like a fucking stallion!"

"Ha, yeah. He's pretty big." I looked over to the pool to where Josh and Brian were play-fighting in the pool, Josh yelling and laughing while Brian grabbed him and tackled him.

"I'm guessing this is a new bull?" Jonny asked, towelling himself dry. "Bold move, inviting him to your bachelor party. Does that mean he's coming to the wedding too?"

Rico set him straight: "Dude, he's Josh's best man."

"Whoa!" Jonny chuckled, shaking his head in disbelief.

I looked over and saw Daniel quietly explaining something to Hamish, who looked surprised as hell. I knew what that was about, and although I was grateful to Daniel for saving me the awkwardness, my dick jumped a little at the idea that one more of my friends had just found out I was a cuckold.

Ben sidled up to me and gestured I follow him into the house, so I excused myself from the conversation. When we were safely inside and out of earshot of everyone else he asked me, "So this Brian guy is like, a regular?"

"Yeah." For a moment I debated trying to make up some kind of story to soften the details a bit, so this wouldn't seem so fucked up to him. But I figured he'd already seen enough, and he'd probably see and hear worse tonight, so I might as well just be honest. "He and Josh have been hooking up for a few months now."

"And you're okay with that?"

"Yeah, it's totally fine. I'm into it. It's, ah, kind of a kink of mine."

He looked confused. "Okay, I get it, everyone's got their things. But at your bachelor party? In front of all your friends? That must be humiliating! It seems fucked up they'd do this to you. Are you sure they're not pushing this too far?"

"No, it's okay. I mean, most of the guys already know."

He shook his head. "It seems a little disrespectful. Why did you guys even invite this guy?"

"Well, I mean, he's the best man."

"What the fuck? The guy who's fucking your soon-to-be husband is the best man?" He looked astonished. "That is some fucked up shit right there."

"Honestly Ben! It's fine!" I was getting a little pissed at his judgmental tone now. "I'm into it. I'm a fucking cuckold. I get off on Brian fucking my boyfriend!"

I heard a few chuckles, and realised I'd raised my voice a bit louder than I'd expected just then. I looked over and saw pretty much everyone looking over at us. One or two were wincing on my behalf. Others were grinning, obviously amused. Including Brian and Josh, sitting in the pool leaning on the edge.

"Hey boy," Brian said to Josh. Loudly, so I could hear. "You hear that? He can't stop talking about how much he loves it when we fuck. You think maybe we should give him a treat?"

"Yeah," Josh replied, wrapping his arms around Brian and planting a kiss on him.

Brian hoisted Josh up, grabbing his ass to support his weight as Josh wrapped his legs around Brian's torso and his arms around his neck. He walked him over to the shallow end of the pool, and gently set him down onto the tiles that edged the pool. He kissed him, leaned over him and gently pushed him onto his back on the pavers. Then he slowly started to peel off his wet swimming briefs, which got a holler from the other guys.

I could see Brian start to get hard. He was standing in water that was only thigh-deep now, and in his wet trunks you could make out the entire outline of his steadily thickening cock, and his full balls. He started to pull his trunks down. "You want my dick, boy?" he asked.

"Yes please!" Josh whimpered.

He pulled his trunks right down and stepped out of them in the water, his beefy cock springing out fully erect. He spit on his hand, rubbed it all over his cock, and then slowly, in front of the whole party, began to slide it into Josh's willing ass.

"Fuck, daddy!" Josh moaned. "It feels so fucking good."

There were some shocked mutters, a little laughter. But it was only a second before Rico and Hassan started to chant "Fuck him, fuck him, fuck him!" as Brian slid the length of his cock all the way in.

Everyone started to crowd around for a better look. Ben looked at me though, astonished. "You're sure? You're sure you're okay with this bro?"

Jonny turned around from the show. "Of course he is man, look how hard he's getting."

They were both staring at me as my erection grew — nowhere near the size of Brian's but obvious enough in my tiny tight swimming trunks.

Ben laughed, but then quickly stifled it. He shrugged his shoulders. "Okay then bro, looks like you're into it."

The guys kept egging Josh and Brian on as they fucked on the edge of the pool. Josh lay back on the wet concrete as Brian slowly sunk his big dick in, drew it out, and sunk it in again rhythmically. Seeing Josh empaled on Brian's cock like that, with all my closest friends as an audience, made me hard beyond belief. It was a strange feeling, feeling my dick grow fully hard unimpeded after so long locked away.

"Fuck, look at him go!"

"That dick, man. God it's fucking huge."

"Joshie's taking it like a pro!"

"Think he'll do me next?"

Brian seemed to be enjoying the comments, the attention. That cocky half-smirk on his face that he was trying not to let show, that gave it away. Josh, on the other hand, seemed completely oblivious. Consumed totally by the feeling of Brian filling him up.

Brian leaned in, and Josh rose into an almost-sitting position to meet him. They kissed as they fucked on the edge of the pool, Josh desperately holding on tight and pinning every inch of his skin against Brian, not letting go for anything.

In one smooth motion, Brian slipped one arm around Josh, and the other under his ass for support, and lifted him off the ground again like he had before. He manoeuvred him into position, lowered his ass down onto his waiting cock, and fucked him standing in the swimming pool. The effortless way he could pick him up, hold his entire weight while he fucked him, all without seeming to strain at all, just made Brian seem hotter and stronger and more masculine than I'd already considered him. If that was even possible.

They fucked like that for a few minutes, until Brian whispered something in Josh's ear. Josh nodded enthusiastically, and then nestled his head into Brian's shoulders, arms wrapped around him tight. Slowly and carefully, Brian started to walk out of the shallow end of the pool, still holding Josh empaled on his cock. He started to walk off into the house.

"Wait, you're not leaving us are you?" Rico asked.

Brian grinned. "Sorry boys. Gonna get a bit of alone time." He carried on walking, carrying Josh into the house to the disappointed groans of my friends. They disappeared into the bedroom — the bedroom that was meant to be reserved for Josh and me — and shut the door.

Once they were gone the guys didn't seem to know quite how to act. Hamish avoided talking to me, or even making eye contact. A couple of the others really leaned in though, and kept on ribbing me. "That must be tough on the old ego," Daniel joked, "Seeing another guy give it to your soon-to-be husband like that."

"Holy shit yeah," Hassan agreed. "Gotta say, that's not something I ever expected to see at a bachelor party."

To be honest though I was only half listening, because I was focused on the noises coming from the bedroom. Those moans, that pleading for Brian to fuck him harder, with all my friends hearing it just as clearly as me. I just stood there amongst my friends with a leaking hard-on in my swimming shorts, getting off on hearing my fiancé get fucked for everyone to hear.

Eventually though, the group just kind of got back to what they were doing, the sounds of fucking in the bedroom becoming like background noise to them. They went back to swimming in the pool, sunning themselves, drinking their cocktails. Some of them tried to make conversation with me to distract me from the sounds, but it never worked and most of them gave up trying after a little while. So the party went on as I sat by the pool with my cock hard and aching, listening to them going at it.

About an hour later, Josh and Brian finally emerged from the bedroom, both naked and glistening with sweat. Brian's huge cock swung back and forth as he strutted around the room, accepting the congratulatory high-fives and fist bumps from my friends for the way he'd just given it to my fiancé.

Josh sat down next to me, put his arms around me, and kissed me on the cheek. "You been having fun baby?"

"He's been loving it," Jonny laughed. "He's been rock hard the whole time you were gone."

Josh grabbed my junk to see for himself. "Happy to help," he said mischievously.

After that we got into the bachelor party proper. Drinking games, music, dancing. As the sun started to go down people started to get some clothes on — even Brian and Josh — and we moved from the pool into the house. By the time it was properly dark we'd got through several bottles of booze and most of the gang were well on their way to getting pretty plastered.

"Hey so is there a stripper?" Jonny asked. "That's like a usual bachelor party thing, right? Or is that just for straights?"

"No, we didn't get a stripper," I confessed. To be honest about it, it had never actually occurred to me, that's how unfamiliar I was with typical bachelor party etiquette. "Sorry to disappoint, man."

"Actually," Josh piped up, "I kind of had something in mind."

Jonny cackled. "Don't tell me you're gonna be the stripper!?"

"We've already seen it all, Joshie!"

"It's not the same now, you've spent most of the afternoon strutting around with your clothes off."

Josh put on a look of mock-offence at the guys' comments. "So you don't want to see me naked again?"

"Okay, okay. Of course we do," Jonny admitted. "Always!"

"Good. Because I know how to put on a show." He grinned. "Jonny, hit the lights. And someone find me a decent song to dance to."

The mood suddenly changed in the room. Most of the lights flickered out, leaving the room dimly lit. At the same time Rico changed the music on the speaker, from the camp anthems that had been playing all evening to some sexy R&B with a good beat.

"Perfect," Josh said appreciatively. He got up off the sofa and stood in the middle of the group. For a second he did nothing, just left us all staring at him in anticipation. Then he caught the beat of the music and slowly started to sway his hips.

Josh had always been a good dancer. A *hot* dancer. And as he got more and more into the music he let his hips and his ass sway more, the way he would on the dance floor in the clubs to get every guy's attention. Slowly he started to pull off his tank top, peeling it carefully from his skin, showing off his toned abs and that soft golden-brown skin that I hadn't got to touch in almost forever.

After a bit of teasing he finally pulled his tank off over his head. He spun it round above his head like a lasso, and then threw it on the floor. Shirtless, now in only his short, tight shorts, he rubbed the dark wiry hair on his chest, and ran his hands all the way down to his waist. The guys were all encouraging him now — some just entertained, while others looked like they might be genuinely aroused.

He came over to me, stood over me. His hands running up and down his body as his hips circled around and around to the music. He leaned over me, brought his face an inch from mine. For a second I thought he was going to kiss me but instead he just held it there, teasing me, for a few seconds before pulling away. He turned, facing the others, his ass in front of me. Then he slipped his thumbs under the elastic of his waistband and started to slowly pull down his shorts. Painfully, tantalisingly slowly he pulled them down, millimetre by millimetre, until I could see his buttcrack and the top of his perfect, golden bubble-butt.

"Get it off!" Jonny hollered. A few of the others hooted in agreement.

He let his hands linger for a few more seconds, teasing everyone with his feigned reluctance. Then in one quick motion he slipped them down, revealing a black jockstrap underneath.

A few of them cheered. A couple laughed at the surprise reveal. "Where did that come from?" Daniel asked. "You were naked half an hour ago, but you found time to go put on a jockstrap for us?"

I couldn't see Josh's face but I could hear the grin in his voice. "Gotta put on a decent show for you guys, you know? Didn't want it to be all over when I got my shorts off."

He turned around, facing me now. My fucking god he was sexy, standing over me in that little jockstrap hugging his junk as he writhed on the spot, rubbing his skin. I wanted to touch that smooth, warm skin so bad. But I didn't. I waited for him to let me.

Josh put a knee up onto the sofa, almost touching my leg. Then another, so he was straddling me. Kneeling, he brought his body close to mine, his stomach inches from my face. He lowered his head, as though he was going to kiss me. I craned my neck upwards and brought my mouth up to meet him. But he didn't kiss me, he just waited there. I could smell the chlorine pool-water on his skin and the alcohol on his breath as he teased me. Then slowly he lowered himself down, letting his ass nestle into my crotch. My hard-on was raging, pulsing almost painfully now that it could finally get fully hard.

He smiled. "Feels like he's enjoying the show," he announced for all the other guys to hear. They all whooped and cheered as Josh started to grind up and down on my hard, sore, straining cock.

I couldn't hold back any more; I grabbed him by the hips and held him as I pressed my cock into his ass crack.

"Uh, uh," he scolded me. He slapped my hand, and as soon as I pulled it away he jumped off me. "No touching.

Only one man gets to touch." He looked over at Brian knowingly, and then back at me. "And it's not you."

He strutted across the circle, picking out his next target. Anthony. He stopped in front of him and turned, his ass at eye level. Looking me dead in the eyes he bent over and touched his toes, giving Anthony a full eyeful. The gang whooped again. He slowly straightened up, vertebra by vertebra. Then slowly, tantalisingly, he dropped his ass into Anthony's lap, sitting on him like a chair. He bucked up and down, riding him, looking at me the whole time.

Then he was up on his feet, dancing again. Slut-dropping and rising again, using his ass to its best advantage. He walked over to Hassan, and to his obvious glee he wrapped his arms around his neck and lowered himself into his lap. I could see Hassan's hips move, simulating fucking Josh as he ground against his cock. God my fiancé was hot.

Josh got up. He worked his way around the circle. He rested a hand on Dan's shoulder, lifted a leg up and set it down on Dan's chair, his cock close to Dan's face. Just for a few seconds. Just long enough for Dan to look at his cock, then look up at his face, with a hungry look in his eyes. Then Josh was moving on, stopping to dance in front of Jonny. Jonny got up and danced behind Josh, so close that their bodies were almost touching. A second later they were actually touching, Josh grinding up against Jonny's crotch and leaning back so his neck was nestled under Jonny's chin. Then like a tease he broke free and carried on around the circle. To Brian.

Brian stood up, and the two of them faced each other. Josh leaned in, and they kissed. Brian's hands traced over Josh's ass, his hips, his back. Then Josh pulled away, pushed Brian back down into his chair, and climbed on.

Josh ground against Brian, who growled with approval as he ran his hands all over Josh's smooth skin. "Oh yeah, daddy," Josh whispered as he ground harder against his cock. He put is arms around Brian's neck. They kissed again, as he kept grinding against him.

By now Josh was hard; I could see the outline of his cock through the fabric of his jock strap. As he rhythmically rose up and down on Brian's lap to the beat of the music, I could see that Brian was hard too under his shorts.

"You gonna let me fuck that little ass of yours?" Brian asked. He asked it as though he knew the answer already.

"You wanna fuck me, daddy?" Josh replied, full of faux-innocence, as though he didn't know what the answer was going to be.

"You boys wanna see Josh get it again?" Brian asked, this time to the whole group.

The cheers and the hollers settled it. Brian and Josh just laughed.

Josh pulled himself up off Brian's lap long enough for Brian two wrestle his shorts off, revealing that big, thick, meaty cock standing at attention again despite having only been shooting its load inside Josh a couple of hours earlier. Slowly, carefully, Josh lowered himself back down. Brian manoeuvred his cock into position as Josh's ass came down on it and slowly swallowed it up.

Brian looked like he was in heaven as each inch was enveloped by Josh's incredible ass. He let out a long sigh, "Fuu-uucckkk," as Josh's ass settled all the way down his shaft leaving him balls deep inside. He started to buck up and down slowly on Brian's dick, letting a tiny whimpery moan escape each time he came back down and felt the full length of it fill him up.

"God this is hot," Hamish said, incredulously. "Simon, I can't believe you get to watch this all the time!"

"So much better than porn," Dan agreed. I looked over at him; I could see his cock starting to harden in his pants. He looked back at me, like he was assessing just how far he could go in the situation. And then slowly he moved his hand towards the bulge in his pants and started to rub it through his shorts.

Seeing that, and seeing that I didn't seem upset, gave the others the confidence to follow suit. Within a minute just about every guy in the room was rubbing his dick. Rico was the first to pull his out; it was hard, the head shiny with precum. He started to slowly jack himself off while he enjoyed the show.

Ben looked a little uncomfortable. "Whoa, I didn't realise this bachelor party was gonna turn into a circle jerk!" he joked awkwardly.

"Don't pretend you don't think it's hot too," Rico shot back.

"Don't worry man," Jonny assured him, half joking, half not. "No one's gonna tell your wife if you want to bust a nut enjoying the show."

He didn't, but he did relax. He leaned back with his beer and watched as Brian's thick, slick cock slid in and out of Josh's asshole. By now everyone else had their dicks in their hands, masturbating to the live porn show going on in front of them. Everyone except me: I knew better. I'd learnt restraint, and I knew not to start too early because I'd end up holding a limp dick in one hand and a load of spent cum in the other before they'd even hit their stride.

"Hey," Rico said, jumping up out of his seat, "I've got an idea." He walked over to the kitchen bench, laden with bottles. He grabbed a forty of bourbon and another of rum, and as many shot glasses as he could pick up without dropping the bottles from under his arm. He set the whole lot down on the coffee table in the centre of the circle. "Shots, every time someone cums."

There was laughter, cheers of agreement. A little protest:

"We'll all be written off in ten minutes!" But it looked like it was agreed.

Rico sat down, this time next to Hamish. Rico tentatively put his hand on Hamish's cock, and Hamish didn't stop him. Instead he took Rico's cock in his hand and the two of them started to jack each other off.

That got more cheers. "So it's a fucking orgy now!" Hassan observed, laughing.

But most people's eyes were still on Josh and Brian. Josh was still riding Brian in his chair. But now he was really going for it: he'd picked up the pace, picked up the intensity, riding him like he was on one of those bucking bronco rides. Slamming his ass right down, wailing as Brian's cock hit him deep. He leaned right back, in ecstasy, as Brian's strong arms held him and stopped him from falling backwards.

At that point Jonny was almost about to bust. "Fuck!" he yelled. "God I'm about to cum."

Josh didn't even look at him; he was leaning back, eyes closed, riding Brian like his cock was the centre of the universe. But between gasps he managed to get out, "On me... cum... on me."

So Jonny took three steps towards Josh, furiously pumping his cock to completion. With an anguished cry he came, shooting a jet of cum all over Josh's chest. Then another, then another."

"Whoooo!" Rico cheered. "Shots up, boys!" He messily poured bourbon all over the row of shot glasses, getting most of them at least pretty full, while Hamish continued to stroke his cock for him. He picked up glasses, handed them round to Hamish, me, Anthony. He clinked his glass against Hamish's and knocked it back. I did the same, and the others all grabbed their glasses and necked them too. Rico quickly refilled them, before getting back to Hamish's waiting cock.

Dan was next. He was quiet, but I could see it in his face.

He jumped out of his chair and staggered over to Josh. He looked at me, straight in the eyes, with a look that was almost apologetic, as he sprayed his load over Josh's face. Josh moaned in appreciation, licked a little of it off his lips, but otherwise was completely absorbed by what Brian was doing to him.

Brian had stopped sitting there passively and letting Josh ride him; now he was pumping him hard, thrusting into him. Fast, frenzied. Making Josh scream.

Rico handed me another shot. I chucked it back, slammed the glass on the table. I couldn't hold back anymore. I reached into my shorts and pulled out my throbbing, aching penis, and started jerking off to the sight of Josh being fucked in front of all my friends.

Hamish was next, but Rico sensed he was close and instead of letting him shoot all over Josh, he wrapped his mouth around Hamish's cock and swallowed his load.

Another shot.

Then Anthony was letting out a battle cry as he unloaded all over Josh's chest. And someone was handing me another shot.

Now even Ben had his hand down his pants. I glanced over just at the right moment to see Rico's dick erupt with Hamish's hand firmly gripping it. But then I was distracted again by the sound Josh was making. I knew that sound. That high-pitched, breathy, desperate squeal. "Oh god!" he yelled. And as Brian pounded him, Josh shot his load. It spurted up into the air like a cork popping off a champagne bottle, and came down all over him. Brian was still fucking him so hard, bouncing him up and down, that when the next few spurts erupted they went in all kinds of directions.

The crowd cheered. There was another shot in front of me.

"I don't know —" Josh moaned, "if I... can... take... much... more..."

But he didn't have to worry, because at that moment Brian's face tensed up. Followed by his shoulder muscles, his stomach. He thrust once more deep into Josh and held it there as he let out an almighty growl.

Josh let out a moan, leaned back and closed his eyes one last time.

No one cheered; everyone was totally silent. As though they didn't want to break the sanctity of that moment when Brian finally gave Josh his load. They were all in awe of the way Brian had fucked him. Silently Hassan and Ben both ejaculated too, but were too lost in the moment to make a sound. A few more seconds and I was there too; I clenched up, and with a sharp intake of breath I felt my load spill out of my dick like an overflowing pot.

The silence lasted a good thirty seconds or so, it seemed like. And then Rico was pouring another row of shots, spilling booze all over the floorboards as he did. He handed me a shot. "Fuck your husband's a lucky man, getting fucked by that god."

I didn't say anything. The room was spinning. I took the shot, chucked it back. As it hit my throat I realised I'd hit my limit. I could feel the vomit welling up in me the same way the cum had been a few seconds earlier in my cock. I got up, and with the world spinning around me I ran to the bathroom to throw up.

# CHAPTER 9

## THE DAY BEFORE THE WEDDING

I WOKE UP WITH AN ACHING NECK FROM THE awkward position I'd ended up sleeping in on the sofa. My head was pounding, made worse by the bright morning sun streaming in the full length glass doors, reflected off the pool outside.

I pulled myself up into a sitting position. It made me dizzy for a few seconds, but then I came right. All the guests from the bachelor party were gone, but the debris of the previous night remained: empty bottles everywhere, sticky patches of spilled drinks on tabletops and counters, bowls of food sitting uneaten, clothing strewn across the floor. With a sigh I reluctantly got up, and feebly started to collect up the rubbish. I went slowly, partly because I wasn't in any kind of state to be able to approach the task with enthusiasm, but also because I didn't want the sounds of clinking glass bottles and bowls to wake up Josh and Brian. Just because I'd been woken up early by the sun it didn't mean they had to be.

After I'd made the house look respectable I decided to go get a coffee. I put on my disheveled-looking clothes from last night — I couldn't get fresh ones without having to go into the bedroom and disturb their sleep — and left, shutting the door quietly behind me.

I wandered over to the main hotel complex. I smelled of stale alcohol. And cigarettes... *did I smoke last night?* I'd ended up pretty drunk and a lot of the end of the night was a blur. I still clearly remembered the sight of Josh riding Brian on the sofa while my friends jacked off and cheered them on though. That memory was pretty much etched into my brain for eternity now.

When I returned to the house with coffee, I found Josh and Brian out of bed. Josh was lazily floating face-up in the pool, while Brian sat on one of the lounge chairs, thick cock out on display.

"Hey baby!" Josh called out. "How you feeling?"

The feeble groan I let out said more than any words I could think of at that moment. "Got you coffee," I said, gesturing with my hands full of takeaway cups. I handed one to Brian, who didn't acknowledge me at all, and set Josh's one down on the table.

Josh swam over and got out of the pool. He walked over to me and gave me a kiss on the cheek. "Have fun last night?" he asked, before he walked over to the table and picked up his coffee.

It had not been the bachelor party I'd expected, that's for sure. I felt a little hurt, a little embarrassed, that I'd been treated like that. Humiliated and sidelined in front of all my friends at my own party, where I was supposed to be one of the two centres of attention. But that just made it hotter; it was a rush like nothing I'd ever felt before. "It was crazy." That statement didn't do it justice, but it's all I could manage at this stage of the morning.

Josh and Brian quickly guzzled down their coffees, then went to shower together. Once they were done, Brian gave

Josh a long — uncomfortably long — kiss goodbye, and left us alone.

"You ready for today?" Josh asked me.

I thought about what was on the cards: our relatives, the small talk, the last minute organising. With this hangover. I was definitely not ready. "I guess I have to be."

———

We packed up our stuff and went our separate ways. We'd decided that in an effort to keep things somewhat traditional, we'd spend the night before the wedding in separate rooms, and not see each other on the big day until the ceremony itself. We were both in the main hotel complex, but on different floors. The first thing I did once I got into my new room was to swallow a few paracetamol and go back to bed. By the time I woke up again, my hangover mostly in check, it was already the afternoon.

I got a bite to eat from down in the hotel restaurant — a greasy all day breakfast buffet to kill the last of my hangover — and then headed out to the main hotel pool where I found most of the guys.

"Here's the groom!" Daniel called out as I approached, from his spot lounging on an inflatable in the middle of the pool. "How's your head?" he asked.

"Not as good as Josh's," Rico joked. "Am I right, Brian?"

A bunch of the guys laughed, including Brian, who was drying off poolside, wearing a different pair of swim shorts from yesterday, but similarly tight-fitting so that they struggled to contain his hefty bulge. I went bright red, and quickly scanned the pool area to see if there was anyone else I knew who might have heard the joke and understood the innuendo behind it. It was only the guys from the bachelor party and a couple of strangers though, so I was safe. For now; I dreaded to think what kind of things people might inadvertently say once my family was around.

I climbed into the pool and swam lazily around with the guys. The cold water was like heaven after the way I'd been feeling ever since I'd woken up that morning.

After a while Josh joined us too, dressed to grab attention in the tiniest pair of swim briefs possible. I jumped out of the water to greet him, and he gave me a kiss. To be honest, getting his attention, and his affection, first before Brian gave me a sense of satisfaction. Maybe more than it should have. It was short-lived though, because Josh then sauntered over to Brian and proceeded to give him a much longer, much steamier kiss, in front of everyone. I felt embarrassed, but I also felt my dick start to get a little hard. I quickly jumped back into the pool just in case it turned into a full-blown erection in my wet shorts for everyone to see.

After that though, the two of them were pretty restrained. To the untrained eye, no one would even know they were fucking. Josh, me, Brian and all the others were just a group of mates chilling in the pool on a hot afternoon.

I didn't hear my phone ring from where I was in the pool, but Daniel answered it for me. I saw him talking to someone briefly, then he hung up. "Your dad's here," he told me. "I told him where we are so he said he's going to come down now."

A couple of minutes later I caught sight of my dad and my stepmother coming out from the hotel building, dressed ready for the pool. With a deep breath to psych myself up for what was bound to be the beginning of a long afternoon of politely greeting family, I jumped out of the pool and went to meet them.

"Dad!" I said, giving him a hug even though I was still dripping from the pool. "Greta! You made it okay then."

"Sure did, son," my dad said. "How's your last day of single life treating you?"

"Better now the hangover's mostly passed," I admitted.

"How was the bachelor party?" he asked.

"Good. I've been paying for it all morning though."

"You know, your dad was a little disappointed he didn't get an invite," Greta told me, a bit of a grin creeping across her face. "I think he would have enjoyed it."

*Enjoyed watching his son get humiliated and emasculated in front of all his friends?* The thought of it made me blush a little.

My dad brushed the accusation aside though. "Not true at all," he said. "You boys gotta have your fun without us oldies cramping your style."

Greta looked around. "Where's my soon-to-be stepson-in-law?" she asked excitedly. She spotted Josh just as he was climbing out of the pool. With wide open arms he walked towards her, and gave her a big hug, soaking her even more than I had. "Greta! Great to see you! You too Neil!" He gave my dad a firm handshake. "Excited about seeing your boy walk down the aisle tomorrow?"

"Never been more excited in all my life," Greta gushed. She was always the more talkative of the couple; my dad was more reserved - I guess that's where I must have got it from.

Josh gestured out to the pool. "These are some of the guys," he told them. "We've got Dan, who you already know. Anthony, Rico, that's Hassan over here, and Hamish." The guys in the pool all gave a wave. "And this," he said, gesturing to Brian as he towelled himself off and sauntered over to us, "This is Brian, my best man."

Greta's eyes widened just a little, just enough for me to notice, and I saw them dip to look down att Brian's crotch as he walked over in his tight, bulge-hugging trunks. "Hi Brian!" she said enthusiastically, swallowing him up into a tight hug. "Lovely to meet you."

"You too. Greta, was it?"

Greta smiled bashfully, obviously pleased that Brian had been paying enough attention to her to catch her name. "That's right. And this is Simon's father, Neil."

Brian extended a hand, and my dad took it. My dad seemed to almost shrink under Brian's firm gaze as he nervously accepted Brian's firm handshake. "Nice to meet you, Brian."

"You too, Neil. You know, the resemblance is uncanny between you and Simon." Brian turned back to Greta, laying on the charm. "You look far too young to be Simon's mother," he said. "I would have guessed sister."

Greta looked pleased with herself. "I'm his step-mother," she explained. "But still, thank you. Such a lovely thing to say!"

I could tell that Brian was deliberately trying to wind me up, flirting with my stepmum like that. It was working, too; I was pissed. I wasn't sure what to do about it; all I knew is that I wanted to get him the hell away from her and my dad. Luckily right at that moment Ben emerged out of nowhere and interrupted the conversation. "Dad! Greta!" He lunged in for hugs and then unleashed a torrent of words at them, in classic Ben style. Brian, having achieved what he was intending already, took the opportunity to quietly slip out of the conversation, but I caught Greta's eyes scan Brian's body hungrily as he walked away.

"You going to tell us how the bachelor party went?" my dad was asking Ben. "Simon's being a bit stingy with the details. Hope you boys behaved yourselves."

*If you only knew.*

Ben let out a puff of breath. "It was certainly something," he replied. "I think you're probably lucky you didn't come, dad. I don't know if you would have been able to wrap your head around it."

My father looked at me, a perplexed and curious. "Well! Do I want to know?"

I shook my head vigorously. "You most definitely don't," I reassured him.

"Anyway," Ben chimed in, "What happens at the bachelor party stays at the bachelor party."

I as distracted just then by the sound of joyful squeals behind me. I turned around to see that Josh's mother and his two sisters had arrived, across the other side of the pool. Josh ran over and the four of them fell into a messy tangle of hugs.

I excused myself from my dad and Greta, and made my way over to them. Before I could get there though, I saw Brian casually stroll over and insert himself into the conversation. As I got closer, I could hear Josh introduce him.

"Mum, Stella, Ava, this is Brian, my best man. Brian, this is my mother, Sofia. And my sisters, Stella and Ava."

I could see they had exactly the same reaction my step-mother had. They all looked at him with surprise, and interest. And I could see them all quickly scan his body from head to toe, taking in his impressive physique.

"Brian! So good to finally meet you," Josh's mother gushed. "Come here!" She wrapped him in a warm, enthusiastic hug that seemed to last a couple of seconds longer than it should. "It's so good to finally meet this best man my Josh keeps talking about."

"Good to meet you too, Sofia," Brian replied, eventually releasing himself from her embrace. He turned to Josh; "You told me your mother was stunning," he said, "but you didn't do her justice!"

*For fuck's sake,* I thought to myself. *Give it a rest.* Josh's mum was lapping it up though.

Ava shook Brian's hand, politely and a little bashfully "Hi," she said, giving him a shy smile. Stella, on the other hand, didn't bother being coy. As Brian extended his hand to shake hers she instead came in for a tight hug, wrapping her arms around his shoulders. She released him, and looked straight into his eyes. "It's a pleasure to meet you," she said, her voice dripping innuendo.

"The pleasure's all mine," Brian replied, all gentlemanly manners.

"We'll see," Stella replied, flashing him her sexiest smile.

That's when I awkwardly broke into the conversation. "Hi!" I said in the most enthusiastic voice I could muster. "Sofia, Stella, Ava, it's so good to see you all!" I hugged them each in turn. They made conversation with me about wedding stuff, but as we spoke I could see each of them glance over at Brian periodically — they couldn't take their eyes off him.

Eventually Brian excused himself from the conversation. "I'm off to get a drink," he announced, interrupting me mid-sentence. "Ladies, lovely to meet you."

As soon as he was gone Stella turned to Josh. "So, is Brian... available?"

"Fuck Stella, you're predictable," Josh laughed. "Sorry to break the news, but he's gay."

Stella looked annoyed. "Of course he fucking is, the best ones always are."

"Besides," Josh added, shooting me a glance and a discreet half-smile, "he's kinda seeing someone."

———

We all had dinner at the hotel restaurant with all the guests who'd arrived that day, one long table full of about twenty-five people. We didn't do the whole rehearsal dinner thing, we weren't into that kind of formality. So it was just a casual dinner with the family and friends.

Josh was well-behaved. He sat by my side, playing the dutiful husband for a change, and making polite conversation with my family. Down at the other end of the table Brian sat with our friends, joking around raucously with them like one of the lads, as though he'd known them all as long as I had. Throughout the dinner I could see various people shooting him glances. Some flirty, wanting him to notice their gaze. Some surreptitious, guilty, like they just couldn't keep their eyes off him. Rico, Anthony, Stella, even my step-mum Greta was getting a look in. It seemed like just about everyone at the table wanted him. But the only guy who got him was the guy who was about to be my husband.

After dinner I was totally shattered. My hangover had caught up with me again and I figured the best thing I could do was to get an early night. So I pulled Josh aside. "Hey babe," I said to him. "I'm going to call it a night."

"No problem," he replied. "I was thinking of doing the same."

I kissed him on the cheek. As I pulled away he took both of my hands in his, and pulled me back in. He kissed me on the lips — long, slow, the way he used to all the time. "I love you," he told me.

"I love you too."

"Now go to bed. And don't knock one out, I want you to save it for our wedding night."

———

I couldn't get to sleep at all though. Of course I couldn't; it was still early, and I was a bundle of nerves thinking about tomorrow.

So eventually I got out of bed, threw on some clothes, and headed down to the bar. I figured a nightcap could help, plus it might keep my mind occupied until I was sleepy enough to actually sleep.

When I got down to the bar, Rico was down there, and Hamish, and a guy I didn't know. I grabbed a glass of whiskey on the rocks and joined them.

"Thought you'd retired already?" Hamish asked.

"Couldn't sleep," I admitted.

He nodded. "Fair enough. I don't think I'd be able to either if it was me getting married tomorrow."

Rico introduced me to the other guy sitting with them. "Hey Simon, this is Todd."

"From Josh's work?" I'd heard of him before, but we hadn't met.

Todd nodded, and shook my hand. "Nice to meet you, man. And congratulations. And thank you so much for inviting me to your wedding."

"No problem. It's good to finally meet you."

At that moment another guy bowled into the room, another I hadn't met before. He acknowledged our group silently with a nod of the head, then went to the bar and got a drink.

He came over, and gave Todd a kiss on the forehead. As he sat down he asked Todd, "Hey, you said your friend the groom was in 204, next door to us?"

"Yeah," Todd confirmed.

"Nice," the guy said, before anyone could get a word in. "Sounds like him and his fiancé are having one more night of wild sex before married life sets in."

Rico and Hamish chuckled; Todd looked mortified and flustered.

"They were really fucking going for it," the guy continued. "You could hear them all the way down the hall." He looked at Todd's panicked face, and realised that Todd was giving him the *'shut up'* look. A little confused, he looked around at the rest of us: Hamish and Rico trying to keep from bursting into laughter, and me going as red as a beetroot with embarrassment.

"Hey," the guy introduced himself, a little nervously. "I'm Alan."

Before I could say anything Hamish jumped in for me. "This is Simon," he said. "One of the grooms."

There was a stunned, awkward silence for a few seconds as Todd and Alan both completely panicked about how badly they'd put their foot in it. Alan scrambled: "I was probably mistaken," he said. "Could have been the other... I'm not even sure now what room..."

By now Rico was openly laughing, and that got Hamish going too. I felt so fucking embarrassed, I wanted to sink into the sofa and disappear. But I figured I'd better confess, so I set them straight. "Don't worry," I assured Alan. "It's all good. That's just Josh having some pre-wedding night fun with his best man, Brian."

Alan and Todd looked incredulously at me. Disbelief and confusion — like I was fucking crazy, being this calm about my fiancé having sex with another man the night before our wedding. But they tried to play it cool. "Well," Alan said hopefully, "sounds like he was having a good time."

We all laughed. I necked the rest of my whiskey, desperate to get out of that situation. I set it down on the table, and said, "Hey, I'm going to leave you boys to it. I need to get some sleep before the big day."

Everyone bid me a polite, if awkward, goodnight as I scurried away. As I made my exit, Rico called out after me, "Hope Josh gets some sleep too."

The whole group erupted in laughter — Alan and Todd too, despite their best efforts not to. I just hurried away to my room, dick swelling in my pants.

*God, that was humiliating,* I thought to myself. *How am I supposed to go to sleep without jacking off now?*

# CHAPTER 10

## THE WEDDING

I ANXIOUSLY FIDGETED IN MY SUIT AS I WAITED FOR my cue. I adjusted my cuffs so they were sticking out just the right distance from the sleeves of my suit jacket. Then folded my arms, messed it up again, and repeated. I adjusted my bow-tie for about the eightieth time, until Dan couldn't take it any more. "Simon it's fine!" he growled. "It's perfect. You don't need to keep playing with it."

"Sorry," I said sheepishly. "I know. Just nervous I guess."

"Of course," Dan replied sympathetically. "I'd be nervous too. It's going to be fine though."

I tried to keep from fidgeting, but it just meant that after about thirty seconds I started to pace instead, without even realising I was doing it.

Dan glanced at his watch. "How long?" I pounced.

"Any second now," he replied.

We were just down the path, out of sight from the assembled wedding guests. Josh and I had decided that we wanted a grand entrance, a moment of drama to start our wedding off like all the straight people got when the bride came walking down the aisle. Neither of us thought it made sense for one of us to walk down the aisle while the other stood there waiting. So we'd decided that we'd both approach from different directions, and meet each other in the middle in front of all our guests, to walk up the aisle together.

Finally I heard the music start. "That's us," Daniel announced, somewhat redundantly. "You ready, Simon?"

I closed my eyes, inhaled deeply, and let it out. I opened my eyes, nodded, and the two of us started up the path. *Here we go.*

It was only a few seconds up the path before the wedding spot came into view. Our friends and family all sitting there patiently, expectantly, lined up in rows of white chairs facing in the opposite direction from me. A few of them turned around, craning their necks to see if the grooms were approaching. Hamish gave me a smile and a thumbs up from his seat, and I responded with a nod and a nervous smile.

Then as I got closer I saw them approaching from the other direction. Josh, handsome beyond belief in a slim tux, dark hair neatly parted and dark stubble neatly cropped. And close behind him Brian, tall, broad, in a suit that could barely contain his muscular shoulders and arms.

We met in the middle where the aisle started. By now everyone was turned, watching us as we were united. Josh was beaming at me, I'm pretty sure I was beaming back at him. We linked arms and started the walk up the aisle together, our respective best men following behind us.

As we walked up the aisle in front of our friends and family, Josh leaned in and whispered quietly in my ear. "Love you baby." Then a pause, followed by, "I'm full of his load."

God that was hot, as well as shocking. Of course last night I'd stroked my cock imagining the two of them fucking in their suits just before Josh walked up the aisle with me. But I hadn't realistically expected him to actually get fucked on our wedding day. But the fact he had, it was incredible. In that moment I pictured the two of them again, sweaty, fucking, just hours or even minutes before our wedding ceremony. The thought of it made my dick start to come to life right there and then. "Fuck," was all I could manage to whisper back. Josh chuckled.

I glanced around at my friends and family, their eyes all following the pair of us as we walked slowly up the aisle to the music of the lone guitarist. As we reached the top of the aisle and stopped in front of the celebrant, we unlinked our arms, but my hand found Josh's and held onto it tight.

The celebrant gave us both a smile and a wink. She'd done this a hundred times, so she probably knew exactly how nervous we both were. *Both? Me, at least.* I had no idea if Josh felt the same, he seemed so calm.

The celebrant reached out her arms dramatically. "Friends, family, loved ones," she started, "We're gathered here, together in this stunning location, to share in the joining of Joshua and Simon in marriage.

"I'm so pleased to be able to welcome you all here, and to thank you for being part of this special moment. Today, two men who love each other with all their hearts," She paused and smiled at us for dramatic effect, then continued, "are making a commitment before the law, and before all of the people they care most about, to live their lives together as one."

She kept talking, but to be honest I wasn't taking much of it in. I was still a nervous wreck. I could feel a bead of cold sweat running down the back of my neck, and my heart was racing a thousand beats a minute. I wasn't having doubts, not at all. I'd never been more sure about anything in my whole life as I was about marrying Josh. But it was still a terrifying moment, the climax of all these months of preparation, with the eyes of everyone I knew on me.

"Would the grooms please turn and face each other." I

heard but I didn't register for a couple of seconds. Then I snapped back into reality, and turned to face Josh.

*God he's handsome.* He was smiling from ear to ear, that same smile that had made me fall in love with him that night he'd first looked at me from across the room. It was effortlessly relaxed but at the same time brimming with enthusiasm and a hint of mischief. Seeing him there looking back at me made me feel immediately more relaxed. A little, that is. I was still absolutely shitting myself. I gave Josh a nervous smile in return.

The celebrant was still talking, but I'd lost track again. I just concentrated on looking straight at Josh, knowing that was the only way I'd get through this ceremony with my nerves intact. I studied every pore of his golden-brown skin, every thick, dark eyelash, his deep brown eyes that were looking straight back at me.

The crowd laughed; the celebrant must have made a joke. I hadn't noticed what it was. I looked around, saw my dad, Greta, my mum, Ben, the boys, all looking back at me with the same kind of adoring look that people make when they're watching online videos of cute baby animals. I looked back at Josh, and that's when I noticed Brian, too, standing close behind him. Almost too close, maybe, almost looming over him. He had a different expression on his face: also a smile, but one of superiority. Like he was in on a joke that I wasn't.

Next, Josh's sisters came up to read a poem we'd selected. Brian deftly stepped aside to give them the floor, crossing past me so he was now standing behind me alongside Dan.

After Stella and Ava finished and took their seats again, that was when they got to the main part.

"The grooms have prepared vows that they will now read," the celebrant announced. "They will also exchange rings as a symbol of their love and commitment for one another. These rings are unbreakable circles, representing the unbreakable bond between these two men. Giving them to each other is a sign of belonging to each other, an always-present reminder of the commitment they're making to each other today."

I went first. I took a deep breath, and took Josh's hand as I looked into his eyes.

"Josh," I started, "You're the love of my life. I've never loved anyone as much as I love you, and I've never loved you more than I do today. You're everything I've ever needed and more. Having you alongside me, spending your life with me, is beyond anything I could have ever wished for."

Josh smiled back at me. I continued. "I promise to be there for you, by your side, always. I promise to always be doing my best for you, for us, even when it gets hard. We're a team, and there's nowhere else I'd rather be than with you. Today you're making me the happiest man in the world by becoming my husband, and I promise to spend my life making you happy too."

I paused, and Daniel appeared at my side, holding out the open ring-box. I took the ring, and slid it slowly onto Josh's finger. "When you look at this ring," I told him, "I want you to remember what it means to me to give it to you. That I adore you, that I'll always be there for you, and that I'm bonded to you forever."

I let out a deep breath that I hadn't even realised I'd been holding in. That bit was over. Now it was Josh's turn.

He looked at me, deep into my eyes, and flashed that smile of his. "Simon. Today you're about to become my husband. But you've always been my best friend. We've shared so much together, and I'm so grateful for you being there with me for it all. You've made me feel safe, and loved, and supported no matter what I do, while still giving me the freedom to find myself and grow as a person. For that I'm so grateful."

He took a pause, lowered his eyes as he breathed in. Then he looked up again. He smiled, this time bashfully, almost nervously. This time though, his eyes weren't looking into mine, they were looking just past me.

"When you came into my life you took my breath away," he said. "There was so much about myself I'd never known until I met you. Being with you has made me feel things I'd never experienced before, feelings I never even knew were possible. When I'm in your arms it's like nothing else matters in the world. Every moment we spend together leaves me longing for more, it feels so perfect I wish it could never end. I never want you to let me go. I am yours, one hundred — no, one thousand — percent."

My heart sank as I watched his eyes follow Brian as he came up beside me, open ring-box in hand. Those words hadn't been meant for me at all.

Brian reached out, presenting the ring to Josh. It almost like he was proposing. With another bashful smile, Josh took the ring from the box. He looked flattered.

Then he looked back at me, and shook off the display of affection he'd just given Brian. He took my hand and slipped the ring onto my finger.

"This ring is a symbol of commitment, fidelity, and respect," he said. "And that's what I want you to think of every time you look at it there on your finger." I could have sworn there was a mischievous glint in his eye as he said that.

"I promise to keep our lives exciting. And no matter what happens on our adventures, know that I love you."

Brian stepped aside again, but not before shooting me another one of his asshole grins.

"Do you, Simon, take Joshua to be your husband?" the celebrant asked me. "To love and honour him, forsaking all others, and holding onto him for ever?"

I replied firmly, decisively. "I do."

She turned to Josh. "Do you, Joshua, take Simon to be

your husband? To love and honour him, forsaking all others
—"

Josh stifled a laugh at that, which made her pause just for a second. He quickly composed himself though.

"And holding onto him forever?"

He looked at me, deep into my eyes. Those big, wide, dark eyes that had mesmerised me the first moment I'd met him and had me enthralled ever since. A grin slowly broke across his face, and without breaking eye contact with me he answered, "I do."

For a moment the whole world stood still as we stood there, gazing into each other's eyes. And then that moment was over, and Josh's eyes flickered away to the side, over my shoulder at Brian.

# Chapter 11

## The Reception

The last of the sun had disappeared over the horizon, and the hotel courtyard was lit up by fairy lights, candles and strings of glittering festoon lights. I enjoyed the moment of reprieve from socialising; Dan had gone to the bathroom, and Josh and Brian were talking to each other in low voices off to my left.

In many ways today had been just as magical and romantic as I'd pictured in all my daydreams. But I also felt a little stung with a feeling of rejection, too. Seeing the things Josh had said in his wedding vows that had been plainly meant for Brian and not me. And then watching the two of them gazing into each other's eyes posing for the photographer, after Josh had asked me to excuse myself from the wedding photos, "just to get a couple of the two of us."

It had hurt, but it had also turned me on like nothing else could. Seeing the look on the photographer's face — so embarrassed for me because it was so obvious there was something going on between the two of them — and thinking about the humiliation of being outed as a cuckold to even more people than had already happened at the bachelor party. I kind of wanted more, but at the same time it terrified me. I could feel my stomach starting to tie itself up in knots because I knew that the wedding speeches were about to start. And I had no idea how much Brian would give away in his.

I was startled out of my thoughts by the sound of cutlery being dinged against a glass to get everyone's attention. Hamish, our MC, got up and said a few words. Then my father gave the first speech. It was fine — a few jokes at my expense, about what I was like as a child and about what kind of family Josh was going to be marrying into. The usual. Just enough laughs, just enough sentimentality.

Then it was Brian's turn. He stood up, and I looked up at him. I felt like I was experiencing vertigo without even getting up from my chair, I was so nervous about what he was going to say.

"Friends and family of our happy couple," he started. "It's a huge honour to be up here in front of you all giving a speech as Josh's best man. We haven't known each other that long, but we've still managed to grow pretty close." He glanced at me briefly as he said the word *close*, but his face didn't give anything away. My heart skipped a beat anyway though.

"I hadn't met either of them when they first met each other, but Josh has told me a little about it. They caught each other's eye from across the room at a party, about seven years ago. For Simon it was love at first sight. For Josh it was... umm... an excuse to not have to catch the subway all the way home after the party." That got a laugh, and Josh jokingly pretended to take offence at the accusation.

"The way Josh tells it, he hadn't expected it to go anywhere. But Simon — always the perfect gentleman — courted a somewhat reluctant Josh, until he finally won him over. With all those same qualities that have made him a fantastic partner, and will continue to make him a fantastic husband. His loyalty, his patience, his understanding. And the fact that he would do absolutely anything for Josh. I don't need to have known Simon long to know that's the truth."

Brian looked over at me with a look I was unfamiliar with. *Tenderness? Admiration? Surely not.*

"These two complement each other," he went on. "Those of you who know Josh and Simon will no doubt know all about how welcoming and hospitable they are. It's one of the things that drew me to them. Josh is the life of the party, all the time. He's always up for anything, and always wants to show you a good time. Am I right? Just ask the boys that were at the bachelor party!"

The guys let out a cheer and a laugh. The rest of the audience laughed along too, despite not understanding exactly what he meant by the reference.

"And Simon, he complements Josh so perfectly because he's such an attentive host. He's welcomed me into his home so many times." He glanced over at me again, this time with just a hint of his usual cocky grin. "And he always does whatever he can to make it enjoyable."

I felt my face burning up, desperately hoping that no one understood the innuendo behind the statement. I heard a smattering of laughter coming from over where the bachelor party crowd was sitting though, and I knew that would have got other people's imaginations going too.

"And it's their differences that make them so right for each other. We all know the cliché, right? Opposites attract. Well it's no more true than for these two. Simon here loves to cook a beautiful meal, while Josh... well lets just say he's lucky someone in the house knows how to cook."

Cue a little polite laughter.

"And we all know Josh likes to be centre of attention. And Simon, well," he shot me a subtle but knowing look, "he's happy to just sit back and watch the action."

Josh stifled a laugh. Surely everyone understood the subtext in that comment.

"What they both share though, is a commitment to each other. That's what you saw today when they got up in front of you all and said those vows. Josh, I want to congratulate you, because you've found someone who will put up with all your antics. And Simon, I know you know how lucky you are, because you landed yourself a ten, for sure.

"Seriously though, I am really happy for you. I know that marriage isn't the happy ending everyone thinks it is. It's just the beginning, and I know your adventure together's going to be wild." He lifted his glass. "So please join me in raising your glasses to toast the happy couple and all the wild adventures to come."

Everyone raised their glasses, and applauded the speech. Brian gave me a wink and took his seat once more. Josh leaned in and whispered something to him, laying his hand on Brian's thigh under the table as he did. The two of them laughed; I wondered what they were laughing about.

The speeches continued pretty uneventfully. Dan, then Josh's mother. It was the usual wedding stuff: a bunch of jokes, a bunch of mushy sentimentality. And then they were done. Josh and I got up, and with a bunch of fanfare and dozens of cellphone cameras pointing at us to catch the moment, we cut the cake.

"Now it's the moment we've all been waiting for," Hamish announced. "Simon, Josh, I'd like to welcome you to the dance floor, so you can share your first dance as husband and husband."

Josh extended his hand. "Will you do me the honour?"

I accepted eagerly, putting my hand in his. "I've been looking forward to this bit," I told him.

Then with all the guests silent in anticipation, the two of us made our way out into the middle of the empty dance floor.

Now that the ceremony and the speeches were out of the way, this was the last of the wedding day moments I'd been nervous about. But I was excited too; these days it wasn't often I got to hold Josh in my arms, scoop him up and envelop him the way Brian so often did.

The band started up. An instrumental cover of an old nineties ballad we'd both danced to in a gay bar one of the first nights we'd been dating. I took a step closer to Josh, so our bodies were only an inch from touching. I rested a hand on his hip, and wrapped the other arm around him so my hand rested on his lower back. He looked into my eyes and smiled, but didn't say a word. With the arm that was wrapped around him I pulled him close, and held him firmly.

Josh rested his head onto my shoulder as the two of us started to gently sway in time to the movement. I led us with slow steps, and he followed instinctively.

"I love you," I whispered in his ear. "So much."

"Me too, baby," he said back.

For a couple of minutes only the two of us existed. No Brian. No family. No crowd of my friends that I'd just humiliated myself in front of two nights earlier. No one and nothing else mattered. It was as if the two of us were just floating in the night sky, tethered to nothing except each other.

Eventually I became aware of other people on the dance floor with us. Other couples had come up to join us, dancing in random patterns around us, locked together tight like we were and swaying to the music.

Someone tapped on my shoulder, and I was suddenly brought out of my haze. I released my hold of Josh and turned to see who it was.

"Mind if I cut in?" It was Brian.

I felt the frown form on my face. *Too fucking soon*, I thought to myself. The first song hasn't even finished yet.

But before I could say anything Josh broke away from me

and enthusiastically latched himself onto Brian. "Certainly," he answered on my behalf.

As I watched helplessly, the two of them started to slow-dance together, and Josh rested his head on Brian's broad chest the same way he'd just been resting it on my shoulder a few seconds earlier.

I stood there for a bit, watching them share this intimate moment in the middle of a dance floor full of my friends and family. Then, feeling the embarrassment well up again, I scanned around the room to see if anyone had noticed. Thankfully, no one seemed to be paying attention. Everyone dancing was too involved in their own moment, and the other dancers had mostly obscured Brian, Josh and I from the view of the rest of the room. I saw my mother looking at me though, her brow furrowed in a look of concern.

I made a retreat from the dance floor as swiftly as I could, hoping no one would notice anything. As I headed for my table my mother intercepted me though. I could tell she was going to say something about what just happened, so I tried to pre-emptively change the conversation. "Mum!" I gave her a big, solid hug. "I haven't even had a chance to talk to you yet, today's been so mad. I'm so glad you ended up being able to make it in time."

"Simon, my baby," she said, squeezing me tight. "I wouldn't miss this for all the world. Congratulations. The ceremony was beautiful."

We released each other from our bearhug. My mum eyed me up suspiciously. "What's the deal with him?" she asked.

"Who?" I asked innocently.

She looked at me with a *'don't try to give me that'* kind of a look. "The best man. The one who just cut you out of your first dance."

I tried to act nonchalant but I knew it wasn't working.

"They're good friends," I said. "I just figured he'd like a turn at dancing with the groom."

My mother didn't look convinced. "Simon, be careful with him," she told me. I could hear the concern in her voice. "That looks like an awfully close friendship."

"Don't worry, mum," I said unconvincingly. I excused myself and headed for the bar, desperate to avoid that topic of conversation. I felt her frown follow me as I did.

For the next half hour or so I worked the room, mingling and making sure I caught up with each guest at least once to make them feel like I actually noticed they'd turned up. I kept an eye on Josh and Brian though; they hadn't left the dance floor the whole time. They were locked together, Josh's head still resting on Brian's chest, looking to all the world like they were the ones who'd just gotten married. It hurt like hell seeing them like that, but every time I looked at them my dick would start to tingle and swell, and I'd have to look away before I got too hard in my suit trousers.

Everyone had noticed by now, I could tell that by the way they'd all avoid looking over at them at all costs while talking to me. All except Jonny, he just came right out and said it: "Dude, that must be rough as hell."

"Huh?" I pretended not to understand what he was talking about.

"Watching Josh with him like that. At your wedding, in front of everyone."

The words *in front of everyone* made my dick jump a bit. "Do you think people realise?"

"Dude. Of course they do."

I guess up until that moment I'd been worried that a few people had twigged onto what was going on. But that was the moment it finally sunk in that everyone knew now. It was crystal clear to everyone I knew that I'd been made a cuckold by my best man. It felt crushing, but exhilarating at the same time. They all knew I'd been bested by Brian, but did they also realise how much it turned me on? If they did they'd think I was a fucking pervert.

I guess I was a fucking pervert.

"Do you want me to say something?" Jonny asked. "I could ask them to stop. I could just interrupt them somehow. I could hit on Brian, maybe." That last suggestion had a hint of hopefulness to it.

I shook my head. "It's fine," I told him.

The band — thank god — finally started to up the tempo on their music, into songs that were no longer any good for slow-dancing. The couples started to split apart on the dance floor, and finally, mercifully, Josh and Brian did the same. Within a couple of minutes the dance floor was just a crowd of people flailing around to the music, and the intimate spectacle of Josh and Brian dancing together was over. The damage was done by now though; everyone had seen it and understood what was going on. I continued to circulate around the guests who weren't dancing, and everyone else respectfully avoided the topic of my husband's romance with the best man.

I was chatting to my dad and his wife when we were interrupted by Josh, who suddenly turned up with two plates of wedding cake. He thrust one at me. "Baby, you gonna try the cake?"

I took the plate.

"Eat up, because I wanna blow this joint."

"You want to go back to our room?"

He nodded enthusiastically. "Hell yes."

"Okay." I wolfed down the cake in about three mouthfuls, desperate not to hold things up. I could feel my dick start to stir already, roused by the prospect of finally getting to fuck my husband for the first time in months. "Okay, lets go."

Josh grinned, and grabbed me by the hand. Then he gestured over to Brian. "Come on," he told him. "Time to go."

"Wait. Brian's coming?"

Josh looked confused. "Of course he is. Did you think it was just going to be us two?"

This whole time I'd been assuming our wedding night would be just the two of us. Even though I'd jerked off a bunch of times to the idea of Brian cuckolding me on my wedding night, I'd always told myself that it was just a fantasy — one that would be way too fucked up to actually happen in real life. I realised then though, that I'd never checked what Josh had been expecting. If I was honest with myself, that was probably because I was too afraid of what he might say. So I'd buried my head in the sand, and now was the moment I had to face the prospect of sharing my husband with Brian tonight.

"It's our wedding night," I pleaded. I could hear how whiny my voice sounded.

"Exactly," Josh replied. "It's my wedding night, so you want me to get fucked properly, right? So come on. I want you to see your *husband* take his first load."

# Chapter 12

## The Wedding Night

We stood outside the door to our little beach hut. "This is it," I said, kind of redundantly. "The wedding night." I pulled out the key from my jacket pocket, and nervously fumbled with it in the lock. With a click it was unlocked, and I pushed the door open to reveal our honeymoon suite.

For a second I thought about what to do next, some kind of gesture to make it special. But that second was all it took for Brian to usurp my big moment. With one smooth motion he scooped Josh up off the ground, one arm under his knees, the other supporting his back. With Josh wrapping an arm around his shoulder and looking adoringly up at his face, Brian carried him across the threshold into our room.

"Hey!" I started to protest, but I stopped when I realised there was no point.

Effortlessly Brian carried Josh across the room and threw him down on the bed. Then he leaned in, climbed onto him, and the two of them made out on the bed as they started to remove their suits.

I followed them into the room and stood, watching. Part

of me was angry, and part of me was hurt. This was our wedding night. This was supposed to be *our* moment: close, intimate, alone together properly for the first time in forever. But the fact that Brian was taking it away from me so callously sent a rush of blood to my cock and made it come alive.

The two of them were completely consumed by each other; all the lust they had kept pent up all day long in front of our wedding guests was all coming out. "Daddy," Josh whimpered, "I've needed this so bad. Fuck, all day looking at you and not being able to have you, it was torture."

"I'm here now, boy," Brian reassured him. "I'm gonna give you what you need."

So this was it then. Brian was going to take my wedding night from me and make it his, while I just stood there and watched. I don't know why I'd expected it to be any different. I just stood there, in my suit, as though I was still standing in front of the celebrant waiting to be married. All the while my husband and his best man tore each other's clothes off and made out on the bed of my honeymoon suite.

Soon Josh's shirt and trousers were gone, and he was stripped down to his underwear, his hard cock straining to get out. Brian had lost his jacket, his tie. His shirt was unbuttoned the whole way down and his powerful chest was pinned against Josh's as he kissed his neck and caressed his ass.

Josh had his eyes closed, in pure pleasure. But his eyelids flickered open for just a moment, and seeing me there must have reminded him of what tonight was supposed to be about . He gently pushed Brian off him, and silently gestured towards me with his eyes.

Brian turned to face me. It was the first time he seemed to remember I was there. The first time either of them had.

"You enjoying your wedding night so far?" he asked. With that smirk, that arrogant fucking smirk that he always had.

"I think he is," Josh said in a feigned whisper. "Look at that tent in his trousers."

Brian looked at my crotch, brow furrowed. "What tent? He doesn't look hard to me."

My face went red with embarrassment. He knew I was fully hard, he just wanted to hammer the point home that my dick was completely inferior.

"Cuck, I asked if you were enjoying your wedding night."

I nodded. "Yes. I am. It's just..."

"It's just what?" Brian demanded.

"I just, I just had kind of thought Josh and I would spend it together. You know, like, alone."

"Aww baby," Josh said. "That's so cute."

"Did you think I was gonna leave my boy unsatisfied on his wedding night?" Brian asked.

*Maybe I could satisfy him,* I thought to myself. *If he ever gave me the chance to try.*

"It is your wedding night though," Brian continued. "So we talked about it earlier and decided it was only fair you be included."

"Properly included," Josh added, with a sympathetic grin.

My heart jumped. So did my dick. "What do you mean?" I asked, giving my desperation away.

"You'll find out," Josh replied. "I wanted to make it special for you, you know?"

"You know what you can do to start?" Brian asked. "Get me some lube."

I hurried over to our bags, which were still all packed and sitting in a cluster over by the door. I was so flustered I couldn't quite remember where the lube would be. I knew I'd brought some — I'd made sure of it, with the intention that I was going to finally have the opportunity to fuck my husband on this trip. Is it with my toiletries? In with my wedding day stuff?

"Hurry the fuck up," Brian demanded. He'd gotten up and was standing by the bed, pulling off the rest of his clothes.

*Oh god, where the fuck is it?* I unzipped my main bag and started flinging things aside searching for the bottle of lube. Couldn't find it anywhere. Unzipped a second bag.

"Baby please," Josh was nagging me. "I need to get fucked."

I pulled things out and threw them aside. Still nothing. *For fuck's sake.* Another bag. Nothing. Maybe Josh would have some. I went for his bag, the one containing his toiletries. And of course, lube was the first thing I came across at the top of the bag. Josh was always prepared for a fuck.

I breathed a massive sigh of relief and brought the lube bottle over to the bed.

By now Josh was completely naked, lying back on the bed hard and ready. Brian was standing before him, naked except for his underwear, the cotton straining with the force of his thick, heavy cock trying to stand up.

"You ready, boy?" he asked Josh.

Josh nodded. "Please fuck me."

Brian turned to me. "You ready?" he asked. "You ready to see me consummate your marriage?"

I blushed red as I nodded.

"I didn't hear you."

I looked straight at my new husband as I answered, "Yes, I'm ready."

"You want this?"

"Yes."

"You want me to be the one that consummates your marriage?"

"Yes."

"Say it."

I scowled at him.

"Say it."

I took a deep breath. "I want you to consummate my marriage."

"Why?"

I didn't know how to answer that.

"Tell me why I'm the one who should be consummating your marriage."

I thought about it for a few seconds. Why did I want him to do this? It was so fucked up. I'd wanted to spend tonight with my husband, alone, free of Brian for once. Why the fuck was I going along with this? Why did it seem so right?

He repeated the question. "Tell me why."

"Because he wants you more," I blurted out. "Because I can't satisfy him the way you do. Because all day long he's been going through this ritual of marrying me, but he's been counting down the hours for you to fuck him."

Brian smiled. "And why do you think I can satisfy him better than you?"

"Because you're superior. You're better than me."

"That's right," he said, nodding. "That's why they call me the Best Man."

I looked at Josh. He'd said nothing this whole time. I thought he'd look awkward, like he felt bad for me. But he was just smiling contentedly, as though everything was just the way it should be. I felt so fucking stupid in that moment, declaring my unworthiness for him right in front of him, right after he'd gone and married me. And he'd never stood up for me, never disagreed, because he knew everything I said was true.

"Take a look at my cock," Brian ordered. I looked; it had gotten bigger, thicker. Hearing me belittle myself like that in front of him was turning him on even more.

"You can lube it up," he told me. "If you want to."

I nodded silently. I wanted to. He'd only ever let me do it that one time before, and ever since then I'd imagined the feel of it every time I thought about him fucking Josh. It had been such a long time that I wasn't sure anymore that the sensation I imagined even resembled the sensation it really felt like. I longed to touch it again.

I started to pour some lube out into my hand, but he stopped me. "No," he said. "Not that hand. Use the hand with your wedding ring on it."

I did what I was told. I poured the lube out onto the palm of my left hand. Then tentatively I reached out, for his cock, the whole time wondering if he was about to stop me and reveal it was just a cruel joke. But he didn't stop me, and I slowly wrapped my hand around it.

It was just as rigid as I remembered it, and full of heat. That big, hard cock, perfect enough that it could be used as a model for a dildo. Slowly I massaged lube up and down the thick shaft of it, feeling the electricity in my own cock as I watched my wedding ring slide along the veiny flesh and accumulate a layer of slick, sticky lube. God it was fucking hot, watching my ring hand wrapped around his cock, knowing that he'd ordered me to do it like that just so I could suffer the humiliation of seeing my new wedding ring covered in the very lube that was going to help him penetrate my husband. On the wedding night fuck that should have been mine.

I lingered on his cock for a little too long, but finally removed my hand. I squeezed out a bit more onto my fingers, and rubbed it all over Josh's waiting hole. He moaned in appreciation, and anticipation.

When they were both fully lubed up, I stepped back respectfully, giving them their space. Brian looked at me. For a moment he said nothing, but then a cocky, menacing grin spread across his face. I didn't know what was coming next, but I knew it couldn't be good.

"Is this what you pictured for your wedding night?" he asked me.

I shook my head. I'd fantasised about being cucked on my

wedding night, of course I had. But I'd never even contemplated the idea that it would actually happen. It was hard, knowing that Brian was about to take this special moment from me. But it was also such a goddamn thrill, beyond anything I could have expected.

"I want to make this moment special," Brian told me. "After all, it's your wedding night."

I dreaded where this was going.

"Give me your ring."

*So this is how it's going to go down.* I looked at Josh, wondering if he was going to save me. But he just looked on, amused, waiting to see how this was going to play out.

I didn't protest. I pulled on my ring — the ring that Josh had put there just a few hours earlier while he told me how much he loved me — and it slid easily off my lube-covered finger. Without being able to look Brian in the eyes I held it out in the palm of my hand, presenting it to him.

"Don't give it to me. Give it to Josh," he told me. "Give it back to your husband."

I handed the ring to Josh, who sat up on the bed and took it from me. He looked at Brian, big wide eyes staring at him like a puppy, waiting for instructions.

Brian didn't say a thing though. He just extended his hand, palm face-down, to Josh.

*God, no.* Now I could see what was coming, and I'm not sure I could handle watching it.

I could see the thrill in Josh's eye when he realised what Brian was suggesting. He bit his lower lip bashfully, and started to slide the ring onto Brian's finger. "Brian," he said, his voice full of mock formality, "you've changed my life. Until I met you I didn't know what it was like for two bodies to become one. You've made me feel things I've never felt before." He looked at me. " Not with my husband, and not with any of the men who've had me before."

Tears welled up in my eyes. And my dick followed suit, leaking a little precum as I watched the two of them.

"Today I became a husband," Josh continued. "Legally I belong to Simon. But my body, my ass, belongs to you completely. I'm yours to use. I want you to fuck me, make love to me; I never want to stop feeling you inside me." He paused, and took a deep breath as he slid the ring that last inch down to the base of his finger. "Brian, I love you." He wrapped his arms around Brian and kissed him, and Brian scooped him up into his strong embrace. They were lost in each other, blind to me standing there in front of them with my dick hard and tears streaming down my face.

Brian lowered Josh down onto the bed onto his back. Josh's legs instinctively wrapped around Brian's torso, exposing his ass. "Brian, fuck me," Josh begged. And just like that, in a smooth fluid motion as though their bodies knew instinctively how to connect, Brian lined his cock up against my husband's hole and entered him.

As I watched them make love I understood completely what Josh had meant about two bodies becoming one. It was like each of them had skin that was magnetically attracted to the other; they were pressed together — their chests, torsos, arms, Josh's legs wrapped tight around Brian — and it looked like they couldn't come apart even if they wanted to. They moved like they were a single entity, pulsing in time with each other, led by the rhythm of Brian's cock as though every thrust was the beating of a heart they shared between them. As it fully sunk in what they had together I was suddenly glad — relieved even — that Josh was getting the wedding night he deserved, made to feel like he was the most important man in the world.

It went on, and on. I could tell that Brian was hitting Josh right in the perfect spot because with every thrust Josh sounded like he was about to lose it. His cries got more desperate, until they became just little breathy squeaks, like he was so close he'd even lost the ability to cry out. And then, in an instant he let out a long, plaintive wail as he orgasmed hard. Brian kept fucking him, not stopping for an instant. As Josh's orgasm subsided he started to pant in time with each hit of his prostate. "God, keep going!" he demanded. Brian kept fucking him, even harder than before.

Brian pulled out, flipped Josh over, and Josh got up onto his hands and knees. Brian started to fuck him from behind. I could see that Josh was still hard, that his orgasm hadn't put him off for even a minute. His eyes were closed; he was in absolute ecstasy as Brian rammed him from behind. I could hear the sound of skin smacking against skin from the force of Brian's fuck.

Josh's moans got faster, higher, more desperate again. *Holy shit, is he going to cum a second time?* Brian gripped his ass and pumped as hard and as deep as he could, and suddenly Josh was screaming again, his face contorted in painful pleasure as he came again. I watched his cock to see it erupt, but instead of a forceful eruption what I saw was a steady stream of semen dripping out of his cock as Brian stimulated him to what must have been his second anal orgasm.

And still, Brian just kept fucking Josh, and Josh kept taking it.

Eventually though, Brian slowed down. Josh, exhausted and wrecked, started to slump onto the bed, and Brian finally gave him a break. He pulled out, and let Josh collapse in a heap.

Brian looked at me, for the first time since they'd started fucking. "Enjoying yourself?" he asked.

I nodded meekly. "I've never seen anyone else do that to him. Make him cum multiple times like that."

"I'm happy I could make your wedding night special," he

joked. He could see I didn't find it funny though; this wasn't the kind of special I'd thought it would be.

"Now that I've consummated your marriage for you, I figure you deserve a little treat," he told me. "After all, it's the biggest day of your life, right?"

I didn't say anything. I wasn't sure where this was going, but I figured I must be in for some more taunting.

"Do you want to have sex with your husband?" he asked.

"Really?" My confusion made Brian laugh; I was such a fucking cuckold that I was literally surprised about being allowed to fuck my husband on my wedding night. "Yes! Yes I want to."

Brian grinned. "Ask your husband then."

I looked at Josh. "Can I?"

Josh's eyes wandered as he considered the request.

"I think you'll need to do better than that," Brian advised.

Now I saw where this was going. If I had any dignity I wouldn't even try. But I was so desparate to finally have sex with Josh again that I couldn't help myself. "Please Josh," I begged. "Please will you let me fuck you? For our wedding night?"

Josh left me hanging for a few more seconds before he finally spoke. "You heard what I said before, right? My ass belongs to Brian. So he's the one you need to ask." He grinned at me, obviously finding my pathetic begging funny.

I hung my head, almost ready to give up. But no, I wasn't going to give up. Not tonight. "Brian?" I looked at him square in the face, something I almost never managed to do. "Can I have sex with my husband tonight? Please?"

The pause was agony. Brian was loving it, seeing me like this; his smile said it all. Finally, he said the words I was dying to hear: "Sure. You can have a bit of wedding night sex with your husband."

I almost cried tears of joy. I started to frantically tear off my tie and my suit jacket, ready to pounce on Josh.

"Don't worry about getting naked," Brian stopped me. "Josh doesn't want to see you naked. Just get your little dick out."

I stopped in my tracks. I looked at Josh, who seemed to find that funny.

I undid my belt, and unzipped the fly of my trousers which were already damp with precum. Underneath my underwear had a dark, wet patch where I'd been leaking. I reached in and pulled my hard dick out of my pants. The feeling of release, as I freed it from the fabric it had been straining against, was incredible.

Josh was lying on his back, sweaty, tired, fully fucked. I climbed onto the bed awkwardly, my trousers and underpants around my thighs. Tentatively, nervously, I touched the skin of his chest. I'd almost forgotten what it felt like.

"I love you," I whispered to him.

He gave me an affectionate, if condescending, laugh. "I know, baby. I love you too. You excited about finally getting to fuck me?"

I didn't answer. I just leaned in, kissed him. He half-heartedly returned the kiss, before breaking away. "You going to fuck me or what?" he asked, impatiently, like he wanted it to be over and done with.

I looked up at Brian, who was looming over us. "Can I?" I asked. I don't know why I was asking him, but I felt like I needed to. "Can I fuck him now?"

Brian nodded silently.

I shuffled onto Josh, and with one hand I lined my dick up against his hole. *This is it,* I told myself. *This is the moment I've been waiting for.*

Slowly, carefully I slid into him. His hole was so loose that I could barely feel anything. Josh didn't react at all, like he didn't even realise I'd put it in. I held it there, in him, relishing the experience of finally being inside him again even if it didn't feel anything like it used to.

I withdrew a little, then thrust slowly back in.

I looked up at Brian, who was looking down at Josh. "What's it like?" he asked. "Getting fucked by this guy again."

"Oh my god," Josh guffawed. "He is so bad at this. Can you please just take over again?"

Hearing that from my husband stabbed at me. But I kept on fucking him. I stepped up the pace a little, hoping that if I put some vigour into it he might feel something more.

"You hear that?" Brian asked. He must have been talking to me now. "You don't know how to fuck your new husband right."

"Please don't make me stop!" I begged.

"I can't feel him," Josh admitted, laughing.

I pumped harder in his loose, sloppy ass.

"I don't know if you'll ever be able to satisfy your husband again," Brian mused.

"He could never satisfy me in the first place," Josh countered. "Not like you can."

"Why the fuck did you marry this loser?"

I came. As soon as I heard the word *loser* I felt it well up inside of me, and a second later it was rushing up and out, spilling out into Josh's gaping ass. "Ugghhhh!" I moaned, full of dismay as I let out the most pathetic orgasm of my life. I whimpered a little as the last of it dribbled out, and I stopped pumping.

"Oh my god did you just cum?" Josh asked, astonished.

I didn't answer, I couldn't admit it.

"Holy shit, that wasn't even thirty seconds!"

I pulled out of him; he still didn't seem to feel anything. I got up, and stood there in front of Josh and Brian as my dick started to shrivel back down to a flaccid state.

"Now that's over..." said Brian. He didn't finish the sentence though, because the meaning was obvious. He descended on Josh again, and within a few seconds the two of them were intertwined again and Brian was filling Josh's ass once more in a way that I was no longer capable of.

Now that I'd cum I was suddenly so tired. The exhaustion of the day — the emotional roller coaster of marrying the man I love and then seeing him so completely in love with another, better man — had wrecked me. As hot as it was seeing them together, I didn't want to watch anymore.

I sat down in the chair across the room, head in hands, trying to make sense of how today had played out.

They must have seen me sitting there and sensed my mood because they slowed down for a second. "You okay?" Josh called out.

I nodded. "It's just a lot, you know."

Josh gave Brian a little nod, and Brian pulled out. Josh got up off the bed and came over to me. He took my hand, and I looked up to find him looking back at me, sympathy on his face. "I thought you'd want to see Brian fuck me on our wedding night," he admitted apologetically. "But I guess it's probably a hard thing to have to see, even for a total cuckold. And maybe we went a little too far making fun of you. You know I love you though, right?"

"You love him too though."

He nodded. "Yeah I do. But I chose to marry you today, remember? We all have our parts to play in this relationship; he may fuck me better than you — way better than you — but you'll always be my husband, okay?"

I nodded, confused about what it all meant but grateful for Josh's sympathy.

"I'm gonna spend my life loving you, even though you're kinda pathetic in bed. And you're gonna spend your life loving me, watching while a better man gives me what you can't."

I nodded. This was what I'd always fantasised about, a cuckold marriage where my husband's lovers would claim not just his body but also his heart, and humiliate me as they excluded me from their lovemaking. It was going to be a harder ride than I'd expected though.

"I think I'm keen to go to bed," I told Josh.

Josh nodded. "Okay. It's been a long day." He paused, and for a moment I thought he might ask Brian to leave. But then he told me, "We're going to keep going, okay? Brian hasn't cum in my ass so I don't want to stop just yet." He kissed me on the forehead and walked back across the room to the bed.

Brian called out, "We got you an extra blanket so you can sleep on the floor." Then he reached over and turned out the main light, leaving only a small bedside lamp to cast a golden glow over them as they made love.

I grabbed the blanket, got down on the hard floor at the foot of the bed, and wrapped myself up in it. And that's the last thing I remember of my wedding night.

# CHAPTER 13

## THE HONEYMOON

THE GUESTS ALL LEFT THE DAY AFTER THE WEDDING. That had been my idea; I didn't want to have a whole bunch of relatives and friends around, all wanting to hang out and spend time with the two of us. I just wanted to be left to enjoy my honeymoon with my husband. Of course I hadn't quite realised at the time just how little of my honeymoon I'd actually be spending with my husband. It was a relief though, knowing everyone would be gone before they'd have a chance to really see the full extent of just how pathetic my cuckolding had become.

That first day the staff kept congratulating Josh and Brian as they walked around the resort. I couldn't blame people for assuming they were the newly married couple. The way they walked hand-in-hand together, how inseparable they were, it seemed like the logical conclusion to make. They made the perfect couple: so handsome, so fit, glowing and smiling and completely in love.

And me? I was just a third wheel, always watching and following a couple of metres behind. The whole time I fidgeted with my wedding ring, glad to have been allowed it back after Brian got out of bed that morning, but unable to think of much else besides the words Josh had said as he'd put the ring on Brian's finger last night.

For most of that first day I still optimistically believed that eventually Brian would leave us to it, and I'd be able have a real honeymoon with my husband. I was encouraged by the fact that they hadn't made me put my dick back in its cage after the night before. I took it as a sign that maybe they'd acknowledged that the fantasy was coming to an end — Brian had fulfilled his role, giving Josh sex that he'd only dreamed of, and letting me live my submissive cuckold fantasy, even on my wedding night. But I figured it was drawing to a close now; at some point Brian was going to pack his things and leave us in peace for our honeymoon, and then by the time we got back he would have started his new job and his trips to stay with us would be over.

I figured I should let them have their fun while they could. I hung back as they swam together in the ocean. I sat clothed by the edge of the pool as they spent happy hour drinking cocktails at the swim-up bar. Then I followed at a respectful distance as they walked hand-in-hand along the beach, framed against the pink and orange clouds as the sun started to set out to sea.

I figured I was entitled to accompany them for dinner though. We all had to eat, and I had a right to be there.

We walked up to the restaurant, the two of them side-by-side and me following. We were met by a waitress who greeted them warmly, not even noticing me. "There's a special spot we save for honeymooners," she told them. "It's got the best view for watching the last of the sunset." She gestured to them to follow; I did too.

She took us to a table. It was set for two. As she turned to usher them towards it she noticed me for the first time. She looked a little confused, not sure what to say. Josh looked at me too — like he'd forgotten I was there until that moment — and he clarified for her: "Oh yeah, we'll need a table for three."

The waitress looked embarrassed. "Sorry, I'll get you another chair. One second." She hurried away as Josh and Brian took their seats. I just stood there, feeling the eyes of every person in the restaurant on me as I waited. I saw the waitress have a brief conversation with someone else as they figured out which table had a free chair they could take. They talked in hushed tones, and both looked over at me standing there like an idiot.

Eventually she was back with a chair. And then a glass, a napkin, some cutlery. Finally I was sitting across a table from my husband, ready for a romantic dinner. Except the romance wasn't for me.

Dinner was the first time I was really included in the conversation. We talked about nothing much really: relived moments from the wedding, talked about the various guests now that they'd left. It was a little surreal having this conversation. It started to feel a little comfortable even. Like all three of us had shared the wedding yesterday. Like we were a throuple, rather than a happy couple and their cuckold third wheel.

"Was your wedding day what you expected?" Brian asked me at one point.

I thought about it a little bit. "A lot of it was, yeah," I told him. "But I hadn't quite realised how involved you were going to be, in everything. And how outed I'd be."

That made Josh laugh. "Yeah," he agreed. "I'd say you're well and truly outed now."

I blushed.

"Do you like that?" Brian asked, his voice suddenly becoming a little bit more serious, more intense. "Everyone finding out by seeing your new husband with me?"

My dick pulsed a little and started to thicken under the

table. I nodded. "I didn't think I'd want that. It was more public than I'd intended. And it hurt, for sure."

Josh put his hand on mine, looking a little sympathetic, and maybe a little guilty.

"Maybe when I'm less horny I'll regret it," I mused. "I mean hell, I'm almost certainly going to regret it. But it was hot, even thinking back to it is hot."

Brian nodded approvingly. "That's good."

"It was a lot though," I admitted. "I'm glad everyone's gone, so there's no one around we know anymore that I have to feel embarrassed about."

"Just all the hotel staff and guests," Brian reminded me with a smirk.

I paused, a little nervous to ask the question that was on my mind. "Brian, how long are you staying for?"

He looked smug. "As long as Josh wants me to, I guess." He paused, then elaborated. "I've got six days off. So I can stay the whole time."

"The whole six days?" I looked at Josh with what I'm guessing must have been desperation in my eyes. "So I don't get any time alone with you?"

"I can leave any time," Brian reassured me. "Any time Josh asks me to."

Josh looked awkward. "Sorry babe," he told me. "I'm pretty sure I'm going to want him here for the whole six days." He took my hand. "We'll still get plenty of time together though, I promise."

"Just no sex," Brian chipped in, with that same smug grin.

———

When we got back to our hut that night, there was a camp stretcher and extra blankets set up in the room. "We asked them to set up a little bed for you," Josh explained.

That night they fucked, for hours, while I lay there in the dark listening to them. Now that I knew how this honeymoon was going to go down, I thought to myself, fuck it. I wasn't going to get any action, so I might as well enjoy it the only way I could. So as I lay there in the dark on the stretcher I jerked myself off listening to the sounds of their lovemaking. I edged myself, stopping every time I got close, enjoying the feeling of being able to hold my hard cock in my hand and stroke it. I managed to last for almost twenty minutes before I came a huge load all over my chest. I felt it trickle down my skin as I lay there catching my breath; they were still fucking, sounding like they hadn't even fully reached their stride.

I got hard again, and once again I tugged on my hard dick listening to Josh moan. In the shadows I could see him riding Brian, bucking up and down, yelping and gasping for breath every time Brian's cock hit that spot that I'd never quite managed to discover. Eventually I came again, while they kept going. Eventually I fell asleep, the rhythmic moans and creaking of the bed lulling me to sleep.

———

On the second day I woke up early. I silently got dressed as the two of them lay there in each other's arms, blissfully spent from the night before and completely unaware of the sun streaming into the room through the thin curtains. I wandered over to the hotel restaurant and ordered some breakfast to go. I could have just called for room service, got it delivered. But it felt more special this way.

When I ordered three coffees I got a little smirk from the barista. "Three, huh." Most of the staff knew by now that I was one of the grooms from the wedding, and I guessed the word must be getting round that I wasn't the only guy sharing the beach hut with my husband. I tried not to let it get to me. I felt like a fucking fool. But at the same time, there's no way I could deny that knowing they all knew I was a cuckold made me horny.

I headed back to the room balancing a tray full of coffees and a couple of cardboard boxes full of fruit, muffins and whatever other food I could carry without it becoming a mess on the way back to the hut.

When I opened the door to the room they stirred a little bit. Josh rolled over and nestled into Brian's chest, and Brian instinctively kissed the top of Josh's head by reflex, like his body knew to do it even in a half-asleep state. With a satisfied groan and a little writhing around the two of them started to wake up properly, while I emptied the contents of the breakfast out onto plates.

Josh sat up. "Morning daddy," he said to Brian, giving him a long kiss. Then he looked over at me. "Morning baby. Have you been out already?"

I nodded. "I got us breakfast. I thought maybe we could eat together."

No one seemed to protest so I carried on doing what I was doing. I brought a tray of food and coffees over and set it down in the middle of the bed, and we all dug in. For a little bit, the three of us sitting together on the bed in the morning sun eating breakfast together, I felt like I was actually a part of this honeymoon.

"Sleep okay?" Josh asked with a grin as he ate a blueberry muffin. "I heard you jerking off last night; hope we didn't keep you awake for too long."

I didn't bother trying to hide my embarrassment from him. At this stage I figured I needed to just own it. "Twice," I admitted, kind of boastfully.

"Glad you're having fun then."

"It wasn't quite what I'd had in mind," I admitted. Josh

looked a little guilty at that, so I added, "But it was hot though."

"Good. Hey, I was thinking. How about you let Brian and me have a bit of alone time after breakfast," Josh suggested. "And then after that the three of us can spend some time together, properly. No following us round like a lost puppy. The three of us — maybe we could go snorkelling or take that walk up to the ridge."

I could feel myself light up at the suggestion, almost disregarding the fact that my husband had basically just told me I was being kicked out of the room so they could fuck without me. I agreed — a little too enthusiastically to maintain any sense of cool — and I hurriedly finished my breakfast, grabbed a book to keep me busy, and gave them the room.

Before I got to the door Josh stopped me though. "Hey," he said, "I think it's probably time you locked up again."

Part of me was devastated, but part of me was desparate to get my cage back on. As much as I'd enjoyed being able to jerk off, and to even be able to fuck my husband — even if it was just a pitiful ten second fuck — it kind of felt wrong for my dick to be free from captivity. So I did what I was told, I locked myself back into my cage. I handed Brian the key, and he put the string back around his neck where it belonged.

I went for a long walk along the beach, my dick aching as it strained against the metal of my cage while I imagined the two of them together in the hut, fucking in the morning sun and enjoying the privacy of having me gone.

After my walk I found a hammock under the trees near the beach and read my book. I'd got through easily eighty pages or so before Josh and Brian found me there late in the morning. Josh bounded up and climbed into my lap, giving me a kiss on the lips and almost tipping me out of the hammock. "Thanks for giving us some time alone," he whispered.

"Did you enjoy yourself?" I asked.

"Oh, fuck yeah," he replied emphatically. "Every time he fucks me it just gets better, you know? He fucked a big load into me. So if you keep your eyes on my ass you might see it leak out."

God, the thought of that made me hard.

That afternoon the three of us picked up some snorkelling gear from the stand down by the beach, and went swimming out to the reef together. We had fun; for a couple of hours I didn't have to watch Josh and Brian touch each other or kiss or gaze into each other's eyes. It was just three friends hanging out, exploring what was under the surface of the ocean, none of us focused on sex. Of course I couldn't help admiring their bodies in their swimsuits; Josh's ass looked so good in his little briefs, and the fabric of Brian's tight shorts clung to the shape of his cock and left nothing to the imagination. But still, I enjoyed the wholesomeness of the experience. I felt like I was actually a part of this little group of me, my husband and his lover.

After we came out of the water we lazed around on the beach for a bit, till we were hot enough for another swim. Then while we were still refreshed enough to feel the energy for it, the three of us headed up through the bush to the ridge overlooking the resort. On the way I was often behind Josh and Brian as they chatted, just watching Brian's muscular, sweat-sheened shoulders as he walked along in front of me. But the order would change periodically based on the speed we all walked, which meant I got some face-time with Josh for a bit as Brian walked on ahead. I even had a one-on-one with Brian at one point, Josh too far in front to join in the conversation. Despite the power imbalance, and despite how much he usually liked to emasculate me, the conversation was remarkably normal. He asked about my family, my upbringing, my life before I met Josh. It was the first time he'd ever really shown an interest in me, besides taking satisfaction in belittling me.

The walk took it out of us — me at least — and by the time we got back it was close to dinner time. The three of us cooled off in the pool, and sat there drinking cocktails until it seemed like a good time for dinner. We ate together at a table for three in the restaurant, and this time I didn't feel like a third wheel. Just like earlier in the day, I felt like one of three friends just enjoying a meal together.

After dinner we went for a walk along the beach. It was a still, cloudless night so not a single star was obscured. The three of us walked side-by-side in the sand. It wasn't till we were almost back at the beach hut that I noticed the two of them holding hands, and was reminded of what the dynamic between us really was. But once Josh noticed me noticing, he extended his hand to hold mine too. So for the rest of the way the three of us walked along the beach, hand-in-hand with Josh in the middle.

It was still early when we got back, but we were all pretty tired out. To my surprise, Josh and Brian didn't even fuck. They got naked, curled up in bed together, and Josh nestled into the space between Brian's chest and his arm. "Night baby," he called out to me. Then he turned off the light.

I was shattered by all the walking and swimming we'd done that day. So I fell asleep almost instantly. I think I woke up in the night to the rustling sheets and low moans of Josh being fucked quietly in the dark, but apart from that I had a sound, peaceful night's sleep.

———

I woke up before them again the next day. I wandered over to the restaurant to get us all coffees, stopping to drink mine on the beach as I watched a flock of seabirds attempting to pluck fish out of the water.

When I got within about ten metres of the hut I could hear them fucking. They must have really been making up for their quiet night, because Josh was wailing like he was taking the pounding of his life. For a few seconds I just stood outside the door, listening to them fuck and feeling my dick straining against its cage, as I wondered whether I should go in and watch or just let them be.

*It's my fucking honeymoon,* I decided eventually. *I should get some fun too.*

I tried to turn the handle, but it was locked from the inside. I hadn't brought my key, I'd figured I wouldn't need it because I'd left the door unlocked when I left. I thought about banging on the door, demanding they let me in. But I figured the decision to lock the door was deliberate; the message was clear.

I headed back to the beach, and drunk Brian's coffee myself. Josh's I threw in the bin, because I can't stand trim milk and I figured two coffees was probably enough for that early in the morning anyway.

I busied myself for a while: I went for a walk down the beach, then a swim in the ocean. I was lucky that I'd been wearing my swim shorts when I went for coffee, otherwise I wouldn't even be able to do that. After an hour or so I walked back down to the hut, but when I paused outside the door I could hear them still fucking, so I turned around and went back to the beach.

I had a nice day on my own. I went for a long walk, round past the big rocky point at the mouth of the harbour. I went on another bush walk, watched the birds in the forest, went for a couple of swims. I snorkelled again, but the spot I tried didn't compare to what I'd seen the day before. I hired a stand-up paddle board, and spent a couple of hours on a leisurely paddle on the still water, watching the fish circling below me.

It was late afternoon when I saw Josh and Brian. I was absentmindedly walking back along the beach towards the hotel, looking out at the sea, and I almost tripped over them. They were lying together on towels on the sand, again wearing nothing but the tiniest swimwear possible. Brian's bulge looked particularly big, like it was close to bursting out; I guess I might have interrupted something.

"Hey hun," Josh said cheerfully. "How's your day been?" Like he didn't even care that he'd ditched me all day.

"It was fine," I replied, a little glum, a little annoyed.

"You been in the water? It's so good right now."

I nodded. "Yeah I've been in a couple of times today already."

I waited for an invitation to join them. But none was forthcoming. So eventually after an awkward few seconds, I just asked. "Mind if I join you?"

Brian looked up at me, a disapproving look on his face. "Dude, can you give us a bit of space?"

I sighed and without a word and kept walking. Josh called out after me, "We'll see you in a bit. Maybe dinner?"

I was fuming. As I walked down the beach I turned to look back, just in time to see Brian run his hand down Josh's abs and under the fabric of his briefs, before Josh playfully batted his hand away and kissed him.

I went to the bar, got a pina colada. Then another. Then one or two of something a bit harder. By the time I decided I should probably eat something, I realised that it was right on dinner time. I figured I should go find them, so I walked back to the beach hut. But there was no sign of them. The door was locked, and there were no noises coming from inside.

I walked back to the restaurant, and when I got there I saw them. They were sitting at that same table we'd all sat at on the first night, but this time it was only set for two. There were candles, it looked romantic. And the two of them looked happy. They'd forgotten about me. Of course they had.

"Table for one, please."

I watched them from across the room as I ate my dinner alone. They were done before me, and Brian's arm was around Josh's shoulder as they walked out of the restaurant together without either of them noticing me there.

The waiter who came over to clear my plate away looked at me sympathetically. "Hey, I'm really sorry man," he said. "It's pretty savage, getting dumped on your honeymoon like that."

"It's not—" I tried to set him straight. "He didn't."

The waiter looked at me like I was crazy. "Umm, how about you tell that to the guy who wined and dined your husband just now. Everyone's seen them all over the resort, and they're looking pretty close."

Everyone's got a line, and I think this is when I reached it. "Thanks for your concern," I barked at him angrily. I got up and got out of the restaurant as fast as I could.

I marched down to the hut. It was locked. Of course it was locked. I banged on the door.

Nothing. I banged again. "Josh! Josh! Let me in!"

Still nothing. I listened; I could hear low voices inside. I banged again. "Josh! Brian! For fuck's sake let me in. This is *my* hut. Josh, you are *my* husband." I thumped as hard as I could. "Let me the fuck in!"

The door opened suddenly, just as I was about to bang on it again. Brian stood there, looming over me, already naked but not yet hard. I instantly felt foolish, but still angry.

He looked me up and down. "Fine." He gestured an invitation into the room. "If you're gonna be such a little bitch about it."

I stepped inside. He pointed to the corner. "You can stay and watch. As long as you sit there, on the floor, and keep quiet. Not a fucking sound. I don't want to know you're here." He walked back over to where Josh was laying on the bed, before turning back to me and saying, "And don't you even think about touching that little caged dick, understood?"

I nodded, and got down on the floor. From there Brian and Josh ignored me as I watched them fuck for the next hour at least. Brian fucked him hard. Rough. Slapped his ass, slapped his face. Held him by the neck as he pounded his ass. Bit his nipples, pulled his hair. "You like that?" he kept asking him. Josh kept nodding. "Fuck yes. Keep fucking me daddy."

Eventually they were turned around, both facing me with Josh on his hands and knees and Brian fucking him from behind. Josh looked directly at me, locked eyes with a look that said *look what he can do that you never could*. Brian though, he just had his eyes closed, enjoying the bliss of wrecking Josh's ass. Eventually with a roar from Brian and a yowl from Josh, Brian came and they collapsed in a heap on the bed.

Eventually they got up. I stayed there, on the floor in the corner as they each knocked back a glass of water, and climbed back into bed under the thin cotton sheet. Then with a tender kiss goodnight to Josh and not a word to me, Brian turned off the light, leaving me to find my way to my cot in the dark.

———

On day four I wasn't leaving them alone again. I was done with being excluded while they enjoyed my honeymoon together. So I didn't go get coffee from the hotel. Instead I just made myself an instant from the complimentary supply in the room, and read a book in bed till the other two were awake.

Josh must have sensed my mood, because when Brian got into the shower after an extended make-out session, Josh said to me, "Baby, I'm sorry I've excluded you more than I meant to."

I didn't reply. He was going to have to work harder than that.

"I thought maybe we could spend the day together," he suggested. "Just us, no Brian."

"Brian won't go for that."

"He's fine. We talked about it already. He's going to give us a bit of space."

I was surprised. And so relieved. I jumped out of my cot and onto the bed, wrapping Josh up in a frenzied hug. "Thank you!" I was almost crying. "Thank you babe, I've missed you so much."

I was half-expecting Brian to put a stop to it, part of another cruel joke at my expense. But as surprising as it was, he stuck to his word. Once he was dressed he headed out for the day, kissing Josh goodbye and telling me, "You look after him, okay?"

Josh and I headed to the hotel for breakfast. The staff seemed surprised to see us together; I was smug as fuck having them finally see me enjoy a meal with my husband alone.

We went for a walk, then a paddle-board session, then a swim. All the things I'd thought we'd be doing together on our honeymoon. Then we sat on the beach on towels on the sand down at the quiet end of the beach, each reading a book, Josh's head resting on my chest. Feeling his skin against mine, in the warmth of the sun, I felt like the day couldn't get any more perfect.

Eventually Josh sat up, and studied me for a second. "I have something for you," he said.

"What?" I asked, my curiosity piqued.

He reached into his bag, the one with his clothes in it, and fished around for a minute. Then he pulled out the key to my cage, and held it up triumphantly.

"Babe!" I was instantly excited. I felt my dick stir and start to swell. "Does this mean...?"

Josh just nodded, and reached for my shorts.

"Babe here?" I asked nervously. "What if people see?"

"Relax. No one's been by here for over an hour. No one ever comes by this part of the beach. And besides," he grinned at me with mischief in his eyes, "doesn't that make it more fun?"

He reached into my shorts, and grabbed the padlock. I didn't protest. He turned the key and I heard the click as the lock released. Slowly Josh slid the cage off my cock, which was already starting to harden enough that it was filling it to the edges. Then he took out the bar that held the ring together, and I felt the cock ring release its grip from around my scrotum. It felt free, naked. And excited from Josh's touch.

I leaned over and kissed him. For the first time since our wedding night. He kissed me back. A proper kiss, not an innocent kiss that you do in front of family, but a deep kiss. The kind of kiss that was foreplay.

He wrapped his hand around my dick, and in a second it was fully hard. He just held it, tight, like he was holding a baseball bat or a bicycle handle. I let out a little moan. It was so fucking good to feel him touch me like that.

"Do you like that?" he asked.

"Uh huh. Yes."

"Do you miss it?"

"Yes."

"Does it feel good to have your husband touch your cock?"

"Yes."

He moved his hand ever so slightly. I felt my dick pulse. "Do you want to put it inside me?"

"Yes! Please!" I begged. I sounded pathetic.

"You want to fuck me, right here on this beach? Want me to just climb on top of you and ride you till you bust your nut in my ass?"

"Oh god."

"Do you think I should let you?"

"Please."

"Do you think you deserve it?"

"Yes!" I whined. "I've waited so long..."

"Do you think you could fuck me as well as Brian could?"

My dick pulsed hard at the mention of Brian's name, even though the question made me feel ashamed. "I could try," I said meekly.

"Yeah you could try." He stroked my dick again, just a little. "You could stick your dick in there and poke it around. But I don't think you could make me cum like Brian could."

"Please let me fuck you, please!"

"Why should I let you?"

"I'm your husband. It's our honeymoon."

He slowly stroked my cock as he thought it over. I felt like I was going to explode.

"I guess you can fuck me," he said finally.

"Oh thank god." I put my hand on his ass, slid it under the fabric of his shorts and caressed the area around his hole.

"You can fuck me," he repeated. "If you tell me why you should have access to my ass over Brian."

"I'm your husband."

"You said that already. Tell me why I should want it. Tell me how you'll fuck me better than he has. Tell me all the things you're going to do to me that he can't."

"I can't," I whined.

"What do you mean you can't?" He stroked my dick again.

"I can't fuck you like he does."

"Why not?"

"Don't make me say it," I pleaded.

"Say it and I'll let you have my ass, just this once."

I couldn't get the words out.

"Say it."

I let it out, in a torrent of words. "Because he's more of a man than I am. Because he's got a big dick, bigger than mine, and he knows how to use it better than I do. Because he can dominate you and I can't. Because everything about him, his body, his voice, his attitude, it all makes you horny in ways that I don't do anymore. Ways that I never did."

I felt my dick pulse wildly, and Josh tightened his grip, stroking it slowly. "Keep going," he told me.

"He's a man and I'm a pathetic cuckold. I'm never going to satisfy you the way he does." Saying it made my dick ache with need. I felt the blood coursing through it, felt it pulse in Josh's tight grip the way it would in my cage. Faster and faster, rushing towards a climax.

Josh smiled. "Okay, you can fuck me now."

But I felt it coming already. "No, no, no, no!" I moaned. Josh laughed, because he knew exactly what he'd done to me. I felt my dick spasm uncontrollably in his hand as I ejaculated in my shorts.

*Why would he do this to me?* I'd thought I was so close to being able to fuck him. But I should have realised I wasn't close at all.

"You're welcome!" Josh said as he let go of my deflating dick. "You should go get cleaned up in the water, you can't go walking round with your shorts full of jizz. Then once you're clean we'll get your cage back on."

———

When we got back to the room after dinner Brian was already there, sprawled out naked on the bed. Josh bounded in, and jumped onto the bed and into his arms. "Daddy!" He sat astride him, lowering his ass onto Brian's crotch and kissing him.

"How was your day?" Brian asked.

"Good," Josh replied. "But I need you to fuck me. Like, right now."

"Hubby wasn't up to the job then?" Brian asked.

"Ha, of course not. My ass is untouched, for today at least."

"Well we'd better fix that then." Brian picked Josh up, flipped him onto his back, pushed his legs up into the air and plunged his face into Josh's ass.

I sat there and watched Brian eat Josh out for what seemed like an eternity, before eventually fucking him. As Josh came hands-free he called out, "See, Simon? This is how you do it!"

———

By our last full day I was feeling pretty over it, to be honest. Every time I looked over at Brian with his hands all over my husband I just wanted him gone, even though it made my dick pulse a little each time.

We mostly hung out by the pool. Well, *I* mostly hung out by the pool. Josh and Brian were there on and off, but kept disappearing. Mostly they didn't even tell me where they were going, I'd just look up from my book and discover they were gone. One time though, I saw them walk off together, Brian giving Josh's ass a squeeze as they walked. And I heard a couple of the other guests muttering to each other. I didn't catch all of it, but I caught one of them saying, "They just got married, but he's been fucking his best man ever since."

We ate dinner together, and went for a walk along the beach afterwards. Even though I was feeling jealous, and annoyed, and just tired of Brian, I still thought it was a nice way to spend the evening. And I felt a little bad for Josh — for both Josh and me, to be fair — knowing that his fantasy was almost over. Tomorrow we'd be going back to our lives, and Brian would be going back to his. And his regular visits would be a thing of the past. It would be hard for Josh, because it was obvious beyond a doubt that he'd caught feelings for Brian. He'd used the L word, even. But it was probably for the best, because this was all starting to get a little out of hand. Hell, it had gotten out of hand weeks ago.

As we walked back, Josh took me aside. "Hey babe," he said, "could you do me a favour? Could you go on ahead, so I can have a little time with Brian? We'll meet you back at the hut."

I obliged, and hurried on ahead while they stayed behind. I didn't go straight back to the hut though. I got far enough to be pretty sure they wouldn't see, and then I headed up into the dunes so I could watch from a distance.

There on the beach I watched them strip their clothes off. They sunk to their knees in the wet sand by the water's edge, and although I couldn't quite make out the detail I could tell they were kissing. Then Josh was in Brian's lap, facing him, bucking up and down as they made love on the beach. The tide must have been coming in; little waves washed into shore around them, soaking them, but they didn't seem to notice. They had each other and that was the only thing that seemed to matter.

I got up from my vantage point, and headed back to the hut. It felt wrong to watch. This was their moment.

# CHAPTER 14

## HOME

THE WHOLE WAY HOME, JOSH AND BRIAN HAD BEEN joking with each other about this "big surprise" they had waiting for me at home. But every time I begged to know what it was, or even for a clue, they were tight lipped. They'd just smirk at each other. The only thing I got out of them — repeatedly — was, "you're going to love it".

I drove, while Josh and Brian sat together in the back. Some of the time we all talked like friends, while some of the time the two of them would talk to each other in hushed, affectionate tones. Occasionally they made out for a little bit, but didn't go any further than that. I guess they were probably exhausted from all the sex they'd had on our honeymoon. It was beautiful to see the two lovers like this. It made me feel a little wistful that this was the end of it.

When we pulled up to the house, the two of them got out. "Bring in our bags," Brian ordered. "We'll be checking that your surprise is ready."

The two of them walked up to the house as I struggled with the bags. I set the first lot down on the front doorstep, and went back for the second lot. After locking up the car I brought all the bags inside. I took ours into the bedroom, and left Brian's in the living room by the door. The two of them were nowhere in sight, so I sat down on the sofa and waited.

A minute or so later the two of them came in from the back yard, both looking pleased. Brian looked at me, looked at his bags on the floor, and smirked that arrogant alpha smirk he always does. Like he knew something I didn't. "Wedding present's all ready for you," he said. "Come on."

I studied both their faces, but other than that arrogant smirk on Brian's face there was nothing to give any indication of what was about to happen. If anything, Josh looked a little nervous.

I followed them through the kitchen and out into the yard. The garden looked the same, and it took me a second to realise what the surprise was. But then I saw that the shed was newly painted, with a new door.

"You got the shed renovated?"

Josh said nothing. "Look inside," Brian said, gesturing.

I opened up the door and looked in. It had been completely remodelled. The walls painted a neutral tone, a new single bed, bedside table and writing desk. There were lights, carpet and curtains. It wasn't exactly how I would have chosen to decorate — the choice of a single bed in a home office seemed especially odd — but it looked clean and inviting. I could see that the tiny bathroom had been remodelled too.

"This is great, you guys! I can't believe you did this! How did you even afford it?"

"I used the money we've been saving for it," Josh piped up.

Brian just smirked that smirk of his.

Then it hit me. The single bed. The fact that they used my money to do it. The way they kept on talking about it being a surprise especially for me. "Hang on. This is—"

Brian stopped me. "You're gonna love it out here."

My stomach dropped. I was stunned silent for a second. I looked at Josh; he looked so pleased with himself, like he honestly believed I was going to be happy about this surprise he'd just hit me with. For a few seconds I didn't know what to say. Then finally I asked the obvious question. "How often?"

"That's the other part of the surprise, baby," Josh replied. "You know Brian's promotion? Turns out they didn't mind which branch he works from. So he's transferred here. And the best part is that because the promotion means he doesn't have to travel anymore, he'll be here all the time."

I felt shellshocked. "He's moving in?"

The smile started to disappear from Josh's face as it sunk in that I wasn't as happy as he'd expected I would be. *How could he have thought I'd be okay with this?*

"Into our bedroom, with you?"

Josh nodded. "I guess it's a lot, It's hot though, right? Cucked full time."

A tear rolled down my cheek. "But we're... we're married."

"Of course we are. You're my husband, and I love you. I wanted to marry you and I want to be married to you." Josh held me by the arms, and looked straight into my eyes. There was love in there, definitely. Pity too, though. "You'll always be my husband. My cuckold husband. And he's my bull. And now we'll both have him around all the time."

He knew exactly what to say. The moment he called me a cuckold my dick twitched and made my cage flail about. And it did it again when he said the word 'bull'. And the thought of my bull moving in, claiming my bedroom permanently, was already making me start to fill out my cage. Even after everything though, all the humiliation I'd suffered the last few days, this seemed like it could be enough to break me.

"Simon," Josh looked intently in my eyes. "We won't do this if you don't want to."

"Are you serious?" I asked him. "Would you tell Brian to

leave right now and never come back if I told you I wanted you back, all to myself?"

Josh looked scared. He was silent for a long time. He looked over at Brian, who, for at least once in his fucking life had lost the smirk.

Josh looked back at me. "You don't want that, do you baby? You love being a cuck."

"That wasn't the question. I asked you, would you be ok with him leaving, if it's what I wanted?"

Josh looked distraught. He looked at Brian again. This time, the smirk came back.

"I don't know what to say," Josh said to me.

He didn't have to say anything. That said it all.

"Josh, I want to talk to Brian alone."

Josh looked at Brian for reassurance, and he nodded. Josh walked out of the guesthouse, and shut the door behind him.

Brian just stood there, arms folded.

"Why?" I asked. "Why let him marry me, if you wanted to replace me all along?"

Brian chuckled and shook his head. "Don't worry cuck, I'm not replacing you. Like he said, you'll still be his husband, and I'll still be his bull. Just the same as always. Just the way you like it."

Then he took a step closer, and leaned in, as though he was about to tell me a secret. "Honestly cuck, he would do anything for me. I reckon if I'd told him not to marry you, he wouldn't have. But lucky for you, I find the idea of claiming a cuck's husband infinitely hotter than claiming a cuck's boyfriend."

"You're an asshole."

"Yeah I know. The asshole that your husband can't go without. So are you going to accept it? Or are you going to try put your foot down and deprive him of this?" With that he pulled out his girthy cock, and just let it hang there, the evidence of why I'd lost my husband to him.

I said nothing. I knew my mind was made up though, and so did he.

Brian pointed to the bedside table. "There's another present in there for you," he told me.

I went to the drawer and opened it. Inside, still boxed, was a baby monitor.

"Open it."

"Why?" I asked, sulkily.

"Because I'm gonna do something nice for you. I know it's not ideal for you to be stuck out here, missing out on all the fun. So I'm gonna put that baby monitor in our bedroom, so you can still hear us fuck from out here."

*Our bedroom.* Those words stung.

"Do you want me to or not?" Brian asked impatiently. "No skin off my nose if you decide you'd rather leave it in its box."

I grabbed the box, tore it open, and fumbled the batteries into the baby monitor. Then I handed one of them to him, unable to look him in the eye.

"Are we good?" he asked.

"Yes," I mumbled.

"Look at me, cuck," he demanded. When I looked at his face, he was looking sternly into my eyes. "I'll ask again. Are we good?"

I looked at him long and hard. The man who had stolen my husband because he was better than me in every way. "Yes. We're good. I'm glad you're here, and I'm glad Josh has you to fuck him. And I'm grateful to you for the baby monitor."

Brian's face relaxed into a reassuring smile. "Good. I'm glad we had this talk. Now why don't you make yourself at home out here for a bit. I'll leave your bags out in the hallway because I don't want you disturbing us for a while. Later on I'll let you come get the rest of your things."

He walked out of the guesthouse, and shut the door behind him. Through the window I saw Josh go to him, nervously. I saw Brian talk to him, obviously telling him it had gone okay. Josh hugged him, then kissed him passionately.

Josh looked over at me, and smiled. He mouthed the words, "thank you." Followed by, "I love you." Then he took Brian by the hand and led him into the house. As they did, Brian looked back at me and winked.

I turned on the baby monitor receiver. At first there was nothing. But after a few seconds I heard it turn on, and a thud as Brian must have put it down. I could hear them kissing on the other end.

"This is yours now," I heard Josh say.

"It's always been mine." I heard the smack of skin on skin.

Josh laughed. "I mean the room. You ready to fuck me in your new bed?"

"So ready."

"Fuck I've wanted this for so long."

There were a few seconds of silence, and then a gasp. That familiar gasp as Josh's ass accommodated Brian's big cock. Then a whimper.

And then, "I love you, daddy."

"Love you too, boy."

My cock convulsed uncontrollably in its cage. I couldn't help from letting out a sad, pathetic moan as I leaked my load in my pants at the sound of my husband telling another man that he loved him. Then I sat there, a wet patch forming where my cum started to soak through my pants, listening to the moans of my husband and his bull making love in their bed.